The Covered Bridge Murder

The Covered Bridge Murder

Killing Karen O'Day

Andy Weston

ISBN: 978-0-9830144-2-3

Cover Art by Chelsea F. Coomer

Green Cottage Publishing

Dedication:

To my wife, Sharon for all the help she has given me in the creation of this book and many other stories.

Thank you to my granddaughter Chelsea Coomer for her beautiful cover art.

Contents

Prologue

Covered Bridge Road east of Bowling Green Ky. – 1920

In the dark of night, the decaying covered bridge looked like a prehistoric beast, its hungry jaws gaping open like a giant alligator snapping turtle. Spanning Owl's Creek on a seldom used road the bridge was perfectly hidden between a ridge of rocky cliffs to the east, and a thick forest of beech and white oak trees in all other directions. Mostly unknown and unused, its isolation made the bridge an ideal spot to commit murder.

Thirty yards from the belly of the beast, snakes, rats, and other nocturnal creatures watched the horror show provided by the shadowy figure of a large muscular man stooping beside a small unconscious woman. They watched as he calmly picked up a rope, threaded a slip knot into a hangman's noose, and then grab a handful of the woman's long hair.

In no obvious hurry, the man lifted the petite woman's head off the ground, looped the noose around her slim neck, and without pausing pulled the rope tight. The shock of the rope touching her skin caused the woman's body to quiver. He doubled up his fist and hit her viciously in her face breaking her jaw. Then, with a savage push he shoved her head against the ground.

Breathing hard through his nose, and despite the near freezing cold, he wiped the sweat beading on his forehead with the sleeve of his coat and checked the knot again. Satisfied, he stood up straight and tugged the rope tighter around her throat.

Now puffing through an open mouth, he used the strength of the adrenalin rush to walk into the muddy creek, gasping as the bitterly cold water clutched his testicles like the icy fingers of a dead lover. Shivering from the cold he continued wading waist deep to the middle of the creek and threw the loose end of the rope up toward the bridge's main crossbeam. He missed on the first two tries, cursing loudly each time, but made it on the third try. He chuckled loudly and yanked hard.

A muffled cry from the choking, terrified woman echoed in the dark forest as she frantically clawed at the rope, desperately struggling to stay alive, to free herself from the ever-tightening knot.

"Plea…no!" she cried.

Ignoring her pleas, the cold-weakened man sucked in a deep lungful of air and dragged her across the ground. With each step he took, the young woman dug her heels into the rocky mud, fighting to survive another second, fighting to loosen the rope crushing her windpipe, choking her to death.

Losing the battle, she slid down into the murky water, her legs kicking weakly, her fingers scratching and pulling at the noose, then finally letting go.

Sensing the end was near he held her head under the water for several minutes. After the last bubble popped, he reached high on the rope and using all his weight pulled her body out of the water. His shoulders ached from the effort, so he leaned against an upright for several minutes to catch his breath.

Void of any emotion he looked indifferently at the body hanging from the bridge and grunted. Then, as final *coup-de-grâce* he crouched down, squared his shoulders in a boxer's stance and threw a vicious right hook to her stomach. A quick expulsion of water and air burst out of her mouth. He laughed loudly and sloshed out of the water, strolling calmly to his car. As he drove away the woman's body twitched twice, swinging back and forth in the gusts of wind blowing beneath the covered bridge.

Chapter 1

Julie Cramer tapped the pencil impatiently on top of the desk. Professor Robert Jones was late to class again and it irritated the crap out of her. History was her passion. Well, there were two things she loved, history and sex. She loved them both. In fact, she loved history almost as much as she loved making people feel good, and boy did she love making people feel good, in ways most people frown on.

Today she had her raven black hair pulled back in a ponytail that reached midway down her back. She knew Professor Jones liked it that way because he had told her so many times as he was removing the elastic hair tie, letting the locks flow down over her nude shoulders. He also liked the tight green sweater she was wearing that showed off her firm, as he called them, fully packed boobs.

She enjoyed this class because of the professor. He was an expert, a nationally known historian with thirteen books on American and European history to his credit. Because of his expertise she clung to his every word. When he was late it aggravated her. She paid her tuition, when it was time for class he needed to be here.

Julie's love for history began at age fifteen when she read the book, *Present at a Hanging and Other Ghost Stories*, by Ambrose Bierce. An insatiable reader, even at fifteen, Julie read everything she could get her hands on beginning with supposedly true ghost stories. She became entranced with reading Kentucky ghost stories searching for anything she could find, until she eventually ran out of Kentucky material. She loved history, but she felt drawn to true ghost stories, a fascination she couldn't explain.

Today, she was extra excited. Dr. Jones' lectures all semester had been about the city of Bowling Green from 1900 to 1920, and today's topic, according to the class syllabus, was the murder of her mother's older sister, Aunt Karen O'Day. She had seen pictures of Aunt Karen, and she looked just like her.

He's late again, damn it! Probably because of the business I helped him start, she chuckled knowingly. The thought made her squirm in her seat. She sat up straight when he finally walked into the room and sat down on the edge of his desk. He was a small man with narrow shoulders, a van dyke beard, and elbow patches on his sweater. He reminded her of one of those Greenwich Village beatniks she'd seen in magazines.

He removed his unlit pipe from between his clenched teeth and moved it to his left sweater pocket. With an air of the overlord of the manor he surveyed his fiefdom glancing around the room, his predatory eyes lingering a second longer than necessary on Julie Cramer's shapely legs.

Then, with a pinched lip and a quick snort through one nostril he began his lecture. "On Tuesday morning, October 16, 1920, Western Kentucky coed Karen O'Day walked out of her dormitory room at Potter Hall. She told her roommate she was going to cheerleading practice, and that after practice she and her boyfriend, Frederick Desmond, were going to lunch. She said that after lunch they were going to the movie theater downtown to see *The Cabinet of Dr. Caligari.* Her roommate said Karen was a big fan of the actor Werner Kraus." He paused when a hand shot up in the rear of the room.

"Yes Mr. Morris?" Jones said expelling an irritated sigh. Jimmy Morris was one of those students who thought every word out his fat jawed mouth was either very profound or hilariously funny. The truth was it was neither. He was simply an over-weight mama's boy who'd been coddled his entire life. Jones couldn't stand him.

"Professor, you said Karen O'Day's boyfriend was a fellow named Frederick Desmond. Was that the same Frederick Desmond who later became the United States Senator?" Morris asked.

Dr. Jones grunted sarcastically. "Mr. Morris, if you'd studied your history of Kentucky when you were in the seventh grade you would know he was the same Fred Desmond. He was Mr. Hilltopper of 1920, star athlete, and shameless womanizer."

"You sound like you don't like the late Senator," Julie Cramer interrupted, a teasing smile on her beautiful mouth.

Professor Jones turned his head toward his favorite student, a creepy smirk worming its way across his thin reptilian lips. "I'm an historian, Miss Cramer. My life is consumed by research. Nothing I've read, or discovered, about Fred Desmond has shown me there is anything to like."

He turned his attention back to the class and looked down at his notes. "We were discussing Karen O'Day. When Miss O'Day was last seen, she was walking toward the student parking lot with a man wearing a red and white letterman's jacket. Witnesses said they believed the man was Felix Curtis, a teammate of Frederick Desmond. They couldn't swear to it because the fog was so heavy that day it obscured their view. Other than the murderer they were the last people known to have seen her alive."

Doris Brown, the girl with the cat eye glasses perched on a skinny nose, attached to an oblong face, raised her hand. "Professor Jones, you said she told her roommate she was going out with her boyfriend. If that's the case, why did Felix Curtis pick her up?"

Jones, obviously annoyed, stared pointedly at Doris Brown. "Because, according to court room documents, he said Frederick Desmond asked him to do it as a favor."

"Okay," Brown said lifting both hands palm up cynically, "but why are we studying this particular murder? I'm sure there've been other murders that had a greater impact on us than Karen O'Day. What was so important about her?"

"Miss Brown," Jones said lowering his voice as if talking to a misguided child, "Karen O'Day was a very popular student at this college, and this week is the anniversary of her death." He rolled his eyes and paused a moment before turning his attention back to the class. "Now, as I was saying, Karen O'Day's body was found four days later by two thirteen-year-old boys who had gone to the bridge to fish in the creek. When they saw the dead body, they ran home, and their mother called the police.

"An autopsy revealed Karen O'Day had been savagely beaten, raped, and hanged by a rope tied to the crossbeam of the bridge." An uneasy murmur spread through the class room. He waited impatiently until the whispering died down and then looked around the room to see if everyone was finished mumbling. Finally, with an edgy sigh, he said, "By a show of hands, how many of you have ever heard about this case?"

Julie looked around the room. Her hand was the only one raised.

"So, you're familiar with the Karen O'Day murder, Miss Cramer?"

"Yes sir."

He tilted his head and forced a counterfeit smile. "The murder happened a long time ago. It was not one the national press spent much time, if any, covering. How did you happen to hear about it?"

"My mother told me about it," she said matter-of-factly. "Karen O'Day was my aunt."

"*Really*," he said with false interest. "And what did your mother tell you?"

Julie took a long deep breath, and said, "Momma told me that Aunt Karen was beaten half to death, and that a rope was tied around her neck, and that she was then dragged across the muddy, rocky terrain, to the edge of the river. She said Aunt Karen was already dead when the killer threw the rope over a cross beam on the bridge and hoisted her up."

Jones grunted arrogantly. "Now how did she know that Karen O'Day was already dead?"

Julie smiled self-satisfied smirk. "The autopsy. Her lungs were full of water."

"Well, that's the way it was reported in the press, how accurate it is no one really knows. The records were destroyed in a fire in 1933." He had to admit he was impressed with his sexy young student. "Did your mother tell you who murdered the young woman…your Aunt Karen?"

"Yes, she said it was Felix Curtis."

Professor Jones laughed his face full of narcissistic self-congratulation. "I'm afraid that's not right! The real killer was her boyfriend, Frederick Desmond."

Chapter 2

Over-looking the city of Bowling Green, standing like a guarding centurion, is the statue of Henry Hardin Cherry a former President of Western Kentucky University. It is a magnificent statue; a dramatic bronze replica of a man who dedicated his life to education. It is a beacon to higher learning and self-actualization.

Ironically, two hundred yards away, on the east side of College Street, a grayish white Victorian house with the letters ATE nailed above the door represented everything but higher learning. The building had an ominous appearance causing a feeling of cold dread to creep into the heart. Its many gabled windows cowed like troubled eyes searching the dark for a soul it could never find. Through the years the ghoulish façade became intrinsically ingrained in Alpha Tau Epsilon lore. Whoever it was that started the rumor that the fraternity house was haunted no one remembered, but for over forty years people had been claiming to see ghosts in, or looking out, the windows of the old building.

Rather than discouraging prospective members, the alleged sightings had the opposite effect. The fraternity had their pick of pledges. So, to make a little money, and take advantage of their popularity, the fraternity brothers printed t-shirts reading *Everyone Wants to be ATE* across the chest. The administration immediately banned the t-shirt from campus. The ban resulted in shirts selling faster than ten cent cheeseburgers.

Tonight, Chuck Berry's rocking admonition to Maybelline erupted out onto the street, the music so loud the windows vibrated. Occasionally, playful screams and laughter would accompany the sounds of a falling object, that object undoubtedly the unconscious body of a drunken Alpha Tau Epsilon fraternity brother. It was obvious to everyone in a two-block radius that the 'Dukes' were partying.

Today the toppers football team lost again, but everyone on campus was still having fun. No one more so than Preston Desmond's fraternity brothers, a fraternity that never passed an opportunity to get drunk and obnoxious.

The son of wealthy Louisville attorney Frederick Preston Desmond II, Preston Desmond III was a Michelangelo specimen standing six feet one with a sculptured 210-pound body. His black wavy hair and his classic good looks (some compared him to the movie star, Tony Curtis) made him a natural big man on campus. His one flaw, if one considered it such, was the fact that he was the grandson of the late United States Senator from Kentucky, Frederick Preston Desmond, a man who built his fortune running booze with Al Capone. It was rumored that while he was in the U.S. Senate, he funneled thousands of dollars to Adolph Hitler. Proof of him backing Hitler has never been found.

In short, Frederick Preston Desmond III was handsome, popular, and loved to party. But not tonight. Although it had been a good day for the all-American, 240 yards rushing and three touchdowns, he was still haunted by the feeling that the other shoe was about to drop.

Tonight, a baffling sense of dread felt as if it was eating through his heart, like the black plague eating his flesh. It started while he was showering after the game, spreading across his body like a virus, slow and chilled, a cold, queasy, metallic fear that started in his stomach, oozed through his veins, and then gnawed like a Piranha eating his soul. The fear was unexplainable, irrational and undeniable.

He shook his head to disperse the feeling and pulled the shiny black 1965 Corvette Coupe to the curb. He sat for several minutes before engaging the emergency brake. Finally, taking a deep breath, he opened the door and got out.

The car, like everything else about him, was eye catching. On the sidewalk in front of the fraternity house he checked the crease in his khaki gabardine slacks, adjusted the collar on the light blue oxford cloth shirt, and then casually peeled the paper off a stick of Spearmint gum. He stood on the sidewalk for a long time listening to the commotion inside the house. The thought of going inside made him feel sick in his stomach. He took a deep breath, paused long enough to take an admiring glance at the car, and then bounded up the front steps, swung the frat house door open and strolled in.

Cigarette smoke hit him in the face like a dirty mop. He coughed hoarsely. Using his shirt tail to wipe the burning tears from his eyes he forced his way through the crowd toward the kitchen where the air felt a shade lighter. He went to the refrigerator, took out a Budweiser, and, using the bottle opener hanging on a chain next to the telephone on the wall, popped the cap off the beer. He took a long, thirsty pull from the bottle. It was cold, so cold it almost gave him a headache, but it tasted so good. He took another long swallow and belched deep and loud.

"Oh, yeah! touchdown!" John Wayne McKinney laughed as he shuffled his six foot-four, two hundred-forty-five-pound frame from behind the cupboard.

It was the big red-haired all-conference guard's blocking that opened most of the holes allowing Preston Desmond to make the long runs. John Wayne, sometimes called JW for short, was also Preston Desmond's roommate.

"Piss on you, JW!" Desmond said laughing. He threw the bottle cap at McKinney. McKinney ducked forward, and the small missile whizzed past him, ricocheting off the tip of Gwen Chapel's right breast. The way Gwen was sandwiched between McKinney and the wall it was like the bottle cap was a kamikaze bee zeroing in on the perfect flower.

"Ouch!" Gwen yelped grabbing her breast, grimacing in pain. She glared hatefully at Desmond. "That was really mature Preston. Really damn mature! For someone who is as intelligent as you're supposed to be, you can sure act stupid!"

"Oh, come on, Gwen," Preston said not trying to conceal the smile dancing across his face. "You know it was an accident."

"No," she snapped angrily. "Throwing a piece of metal at someone is not an accident it's irresponsible behavior."

"Gwen, cool it!" John Wayne McKinney said. "He didn't mean to hit your damn boob, okay! Now, go someplace and cool off, I'll be there in a few minutes."

Preston laughed. "Want me to kiss it, Gwen? I guarantee that will make it feel better."

"Preston, you're disgusting," she spat. She glared hatefully at both Preston and JW and stormed toward the door.

"Hey, Gwen," Preston said loudly.

She paused, and, with an offended sigh looked back and said, "What do you want?"

"I was just thinking. You know, if those things weren't so big, I probably wouldn't have hit one."

Her eyes narrowed to enraged slits, her lips frozen in a straight tight line. "You're such a jerk!" She pushed the door open with a furious shove and stormed out of the room.

When she was gone Preston laughed. "JW, I think she hates me."

John Wayne chuckled. "No, Gwen doesn't hate you, Prez. She just thinks you're a cocky, arrogant, self-centered, spoiled, rich SOB who thinks his shit doesn't stink." He paused for dramatic effect staring thoughtfully at the ceiling. "You know, come to think of it, she's right."

"Thanks," Preston murmured, and for the third time that night a profound feeling of impending doom washed over him. He shook his head and chugged the beer. He tossed the empty bottle in the trash and grabbed another from the refrigerator. He lifted the bottle to his mouth and took a long drink.

John Wayne picked up on the lost, faraway look, in Preston's eyes.

"Hey, buddy, are you okay," he asked. "You don't look right, is something bothering you?"

"Nah, I'm just a little tired. That's all" He drained the bottle, went to the refrigerator, and retrieved another. "I'm going to visit with the unwashed masses for a while and then go back to the dorm. Are you coming?"

"Better not," John Wayne grunted. "You go ahead. If I expect to get any stinky on my dinky I better smooth things over with Gwen."

"Well, have a good time," Preston muttered. He choked the bottle by the long neck, pushed through the door, and walked into a room that from all appearances looked like a preamble to a Roman orgy. Several of Gwen Chapel's less than sober sorority sisters were dancing in a circle around a much more inebriated sister who was gyrating to the music wearing only her panties while the crowd egged her on.

God! I wish I'd stayed home! Preston thought.

Someone had propped open the front door and the smoke was dissipating enough to be able to breathe without coughing. He mingled with his friends, told a couple of jokes, and laughed hard at several. The last few swallows of beer were getting warm, so he tossed the bottle in the garbage, and turned toward the kitchen to get another. Halfway to the door he spied Lindsey Potter moving toward him.

Oh, shit, he thought.

He had taken Lindsey out twice, once to a dance after a game, then last Thursday to a movie downtown. When the movie was over, they stopped at McDonald's for a burger, and then ended up at Beach Bend Park having sex on a blanket under the stars. Afterwards, she clung to him like her spirit had been washed in the blood.

Now, he wanted to be free of her. It wasn't that she wasn't pretty; she looked like what most people think Scandinavian women look like. Tall, athletic, pretty, blonde and blue eyed. But she had two flaws, flaws that Preston Desmond couldn't abide in a woman. One, she had a chest flatter than his washboard stomach, and secondly, the tendency to talk eighty miles an hour without coming up for air. If she grew some tits, and learned to keep her mouth shut, she would be the perfect woman.

Pretending not to see her, Preston focused his attention on the door, and hurried his step. She was a step faster.

"Hi, Preston," she said smiling brightly. "You were wonderful today! I was so proud of you!" She tottered unsteadily, and grabbed Desmond's arm for support, as she did her body fell against him. She pushed closer. "You look good tonight," she said her voice alcohol husky, her body hot, and damp with sweat. She smelled of rum and coke.

"So, do you, Lindsey," he said gently removing her hand from his arm. He lifted her fingers to his lips, kissed the back of her hand, and then positioned it at her side.

She smiled, and then pouting petulantly, said, "Why haven't you called me?"

"I've meant to, Lindsey, but I've been really busy, what with classes and football. You know how it is. I'll call you in a couple of days."

"You're not just saying that to get rid of me, are you?" She said softly, but there was a hard edge in her voice. "After last Thursday…you know, after what we did…I thought maybe we had something special."

Preston looked in her eyes. The deep blue was starting to fog with tears.

"Hey," he whispered, "I think we do too, Lindsey, but I'm a football player. I've got to concentrate on my game. You understand that, don't you?" He put his arms around her and pulled her close. She melted against his body. "Just be patient, okay? The season will be over before we both know it, and then, we…um…we can, you know."

Her face brightened. "You promise?"

"Yeah…promise…" He lifted her chin with his fingertips and kissed her a peck on the lips, pulling away before she could respond. "Now, I've got to go. I'll talk to you later, okay?"

She forced a smile and nodded. "Okay."

"I'll call you, promise," he said.

Slipping out of her reach he winked at her and pushed his way through the kitchen door. Once inside he went to the refrigerator, pulled out a beer, and popped it open.

"Jeez, can I pick some winners, or what?" he mumbled half aloud. He released a wearied sigh as he lifted the bottle and took a drink.

He left the kitchen and pushed his way through the mostly inebriated partiers who were drinking and laughing at the same stupid jokes he'd heard time and time again. After several trips to the refrigerator, his forced laugh was getting louder, his tongue thick and cheesy. Feeling unsteady on his feet he leaned back against the wall, his eyes surveying the scene. It seemed dreamlike, as if everyone in the room was programmed to shout, drink, laugh, and perform primeval mating rituals. He grunted a whispered mumble, "Of course we're programmed, dumb ass. We're wired to propagate."

He rested his head back against the wall, robotically raising the bottle, taking long drinks, and reliving the day in his mind. Every weekend it was the same damn thing, played out like a motion picture with one reel looping over and over. He'd play a football game Saturday afternoon, get drunk with his frat brothers that night, and then have sex with some girl, usually his fiancée Mona Cooper. Every week it was the same thing, over, and over, and over again. It didn't get any better.

He shook his head trying to clear the cobwebs. He was living the dream. He was a rich, good looking football hero who got everything he wanted, and he still felt like shit. What was wrong with him? Why wasn't the fun, fun? Why wasn't he enjoying the dream instead of feeling so empty? How else could he describe it? He felt empty, empty as a hollowed log. That old blues song by B.B. King said perfectly, the *Thrill Is Gone*. Yes sir, the thrill was certainly gone.

"Are you as bored as I am?" A soft, melodic voice asked.

Preston jerked forward, blinking back to the present, and turned toward the sound of the voice. "Are you talking to me?" he said to the pretty young woman standing next to him.

The beautiful creature laughed. "Yes, I did. I asked you if you're as bored as I am." Her voice was like warm velvet.

"As a matter of fact, I am," he said. He blinked his blood shot eyes to clear the fog. Her black hair gently cascading over her shoulders reminded him of a shampoo commercial. Her dark almost black eyes seemed to search into his soul, and then soften into bottomless pools. She appeared to be about twenty-two, maybe five-seven, and a hundred and ten perfectly formed pounds. She stood just close enough to be provocative. In short, she looked like Natalie Wood's prettier sister.

The smell of her perfume made him think of lilacs and roses; intermingling with her perspiration it created a combination that made him want to climb the wall. For the first time in as long as he could remember he was speechless. He wanted to be cool, but the words coming out of his beer thickened tongue made him cringe. He couldn't take his eyes off her.

A teasing hint of a smile tickled her lips. "Is something wrong?"

"N…no," he slurred, "I'm just thinking…you've got the most kissable looking lips I've ever seen."

She laughed. "Why thank you, sir. Your lips are nice too!"

"Then, can I kiss 'em?" They both laughed.

"I don't think so," she said with a teasing chuckle. "At least not right now."

His eyes found hers for a moment before he tipped the bottle to his mouth and finished the last swallow. "I'm going to get another beer would you care for something?"

"A little white wine if you have it."

He nodded. "I think I saw a bottle on the bar. Don't go away, I'll be right back."

"I won't move a muscle," she replied. Her eyes appeared to sparkle like new stars on a clear night.

Smiling, like a six grader who just met the pretty new girl in school, he stumbled to the kitchen, losing his balance twice in the process, and returned a few minutes later with a bottle of Budweiser and a glass of red wine. She had moved to the front of the room and stood staring out the window. She turned to meet him, seeming to sense his presence. He handed her the glass.

"You moved," he said.

"You found me."

"No white."

"That's okay. Red wine reminds me of blood."

"Blood?"

She chuckled. "That did sound a little psychotic didn't it?"

He grinned. "A little strange, but I wouldn't say psychotic."

"Good. I wouldn't want you to think I'm an escapee from a psychiatric ward."

"If you are, I'll take my chances."

"Oh, you're a risk taker, huh?"

"Of course," he said.

His brain was beginning to feel detached from his body. *It must be the beer, better slow down.* He placed the nearly full bottle on the floor next to the wall.

"My dad had a quote on his office wall that impressed me when I was a little kid," he said. "It was something my grandfather wrote. It said, 'as a man grows older, the things he regrets the most, are the things he DIDN'T do. I try to live with that in mind." He chuckled. "I'm also an adrenaline junky."

"If your grandfather's greatest regrets were the things he didn't do," she said pointedly, "then he was a very fortunate man."

Desmond shrugged. "Yeah, I guess. I never gave it much thought."

She shook her head and smiled. "Don't mind me. I'm just not much for parties. I'm more of a home body."

"Then why don't we get out of here?"

"Let's do," she said. "What do you have in mind?"

"Well, we could ride out to Beach Bend Park and look at the stars. It's a clear night. The stars are bright, like deep in the heart of Texas."

She laughed. "Oh, no, a country music fan."

"I do like Hank Williams's music," he said.

"Well, I think it's a little too cool for looking at the stars."

"In that case, we could drive over to the Orange Bar and have a drink in the comfort of a dark, quiet booth."

She looked into his bloodshot eyes after watching him stagger and said. "I've got a better idea. Why don't we just go for a walk?"

Preston rolled a burp grunt. "Yeah, I probably need the air."

He touched her elbow and led her to the front door. The temperature outside had dropped several degrees causing her to shiver. Preston took off his red and white letterman jacket and draped it over her shoulders.

"Thank you," she said wrapping the jacket tightly around her body. "By the way, my name is Karen O'Day."

"Nice to meet you, Karen. I'm Pres…"

"I know who you are. Your name is Fredrick Preston Desmond III. You're a senior, majoring in political science. You plan to go to law school after you spend a few years in the National Football League. You're assuming you'll be drafted, and you probably will be, since you've led the nation in touchdowns and yardage gained, as well as being a first string All-American each of the past two years. You are also leading in the race for the Heisman Trophy."

He laughed. "I like the way you think, but I don't believe it will ever happen. I'm a little All-American and we're not in a Division I football conference."

"I don't know what that means."

"It means we don't play against the bigger schools."

"Oh!"

"But that's okay I didn't mean to interrupt you reciting my biography." They both laughed.

"Yes, well, as I was saying, your grandfather was Senator Fredrick Desmond. He was a charismatic senator from Kentucky who disappeared in a mysterious plane incident over the Bermuda Triangle a year before you were born. No sign of him or the plane has ever been found.

"You are presently dating Mona Coo—"

"Engaged to…"

Karen shrugged flippantly. "Okay, engaged to the tall blonde cheerleader who is always located second from the left during the games." She nodded. "She's very pretty; you have wonderful taste in women." She paused and gave his ribs a playful poke with her elbow. "That girl you were talking to a few minutes ago didn't look like Mona Cooper."

Preston felt the blood rush to his face. "Oh, no…that was Lindsey Potter. Lindsey's a girl I went out with a couple of times when Mona and I took a break."

"It looked to me as if she thought it was going to be a long-term relationship."

"Well, it wasn't," He retorted a little irritated. A frown wrinkled his forehead. "How do you know so much about me?"

She laughed. "Oh, come on, you don't actually think our meeting was an accident, do you? I did my homework."

"But how did you find out so much?"

"I asked around. It was really very easy. All I had to do was tell people I was researching an article for the newspaper, and they would tell me anything that I wanted to know." She paused. "By the way, where is Mona?"

"Why?"

"I'm just curious."

"We had a fight."

"Oh, I'm sorry."

"No, you're not."

"Well, just a little," she teased sipping the last of the wine. Preston took the empty glass and tossed it in the shrubs edging the sidewalk.

He set his head in a guarded tilt. "You know, I've never mention to anyone that I thought I might be drafted to play professional football. What made you say that?"

The sound of her laughter made him want to pull her close and kiss her. "I made that up," she said. "I'm a huge football fan. I know my football, and I believe as good as you are the pros are bound to make you an offer too good to pass up."

"But why go to all the trouble to find out about me?"

"I wanted to know as much about you as I could."

"Why?"

Her brow wrinkled as she paused for several moments before saying, "It's a long story."

"We've got time, unless you've got a hot date somewhere?"

Her lips puckered a sexy playful smile. "No, of course not."

Without thinking he reached over and touched her arm. "Then let's hear it."

She glimpsed a fleeting look at his hand and smiled. "If you really want to hear it."

"I do."

She shrugged one shoulder. "Okay," she said. "I wanted to meet you because, when my aunt was a student here, she dated your grandfather Fredrick."

"You're kidding?"

"No, I'm not."

"Really…?"

"Yes, my Aunt Katie also went to school here, and she used to talk about how much Aunt Karen loved Fredrick Desmond. She said Aunt Karen's life revolved around him."

"I've heard stories about my grandpa," Preston said, "and from what they say, he was quite the ladies' man. He supposedly had a lot of girlfriends."

"Aunt Kate said the same thing." Then casting a fleeting glance out of the corner of her eye, she said, "From what I've heard the apple didn't fall far from the family tree."

The temperature seemed to drop sharply. Changing the subject, Preston said, "How long have you been at Western? You're obviously not a freshman."

"Goodness no, I'm a junior psychology major. My first two years were at the University of Kentucky."

"I thought Kentucky was supposed to have one of the best psych programs in the state. Why did you transfer here?"

Without replying she took his arm and moved close against him. "Don't you think it's getting a bit chilly? I know you have-to be cold."

"Just a little," he said trying not to shiver.

"Then let's head back."

He nodded and swung around on the sidewalk and headed back down the hill. They walked to the front of the fraternity house and stopped next to Preston's car. She slipped her hand from his arm.

"I really am tired. It's been a long day," she said. "I think I'm going to go back to the dorm."

"It's too cold for you to walk. Let me drive you home."

"I am freezing," she said with a smile.

"Where do you stay?"

"In…um, Potter Hall, but I don't want to spoil your party."

"Believe me, you're not spoiling anything. Besides, Potter Hall is right over the hill from my place. I live in Sandstone Manor." He opened the Corvette's door. "Hop in."

Karen looked deep in his eyes for a long moment before moving toward the car and slipping onto the seat.

"You know," she said, "Mona Cooper is going to find out about this. She will *not* be happy."

Preston chuckled arrogantly. "She'll get over it. I'll tell her you're a friend of the family."

Karen's penetrating gaze lingered on him for several seconds before she reached for the handle and pulled the door closed. As he hit the ignition, she turned her head toward the window, and, with a satisfied smirk curling across her lips thought, *round one.*

Neither spoke on the drive to the dormitory.

Preston pulled to the curb in front of Potter Hall, turned the engine off, and started to get out of the car.

"No, that's okay," she said laying a hand on his thigh. "Let's say goodnight here. We wouldn't want someone seeing you walk me to the door…Mona, you know."

He grimaced, and nodded, "Yeah, good thinking."

In the light of a street lamp she sat looking at him, her eyes studying his face. "Did anyone ever tell you you're very pretty?" she said. Preston didn't know how to respond, and then, without warning, she leaned across the console and kissed him lightly on the lips. "I enjoyed talking with you tonight. I'm sure we'll do it again."

Without another word she hurried out of the car and walked rapidly up the brick sidewalk to the dorm.

Still unsure what had just happened, Preston watched until she entered the building, and then drove away. Once the Corvette pulled out onto the street Karen stepped out of the foyer, and stood in the shadows, her gaze never leaving the tail lights of the black sports car until it was out of sight. Making sure no one had seen her she hurried down the hill, stepped into a blue '60 Ford, and drove slowly down College Street toward Main street.

Chapter 3

Preston couldn't sleep. Reliving the game only psyched him up more. Counting sheep didn't help, and neither did counting ceiling tiles. He rolled over and looked at the clock. 3:30. Shit! He rose, went to the desk, turned on the lamp, and opened the first book he touched. Mid-way through the first paragraph the faint breath of lilacs and roses seemed to kiss his senses.

Boy am I hallucinating! I need to get some sleep.

He turned off the desk lamp, walked to the window, and stood staring up the hill at the historic ivy-covered facade of Potter Hall. Somewhere behind those walls was Karen O'Day, the beautiful, alluring mysterious Karen O'Day whose sudden appearance out of nowhere was consuming his every thought. What room was she in? Was she having a hard time sleeping? Was she thinking of me? This is totally crazy!

If someone would walk in and demanded he explain to them how he felt, he couldn't. All he knew was that for some strange reason he suddenly felt obsessed with a woman he'd just met. He knew nothing about her, yet he felt like he'd known her all his life. He wanted her yet felt strangely afraid of her. Why, he couldn't say.

The door opened, and John Wayne McKinney staggered in and dropped down heavily on his bunk. He looked across the room at Preston through runny blood shot eyes.

"Hey man," he said slurring his words as he stuck his hand down his pants and adjusted himself. "Do you enjoy standing in the dark?"

"I couldn't sleep."

"I guess that good-looking babe with the black hair and beautiful lips got you all lathered up, huh. What's the matter, Stud? I'm guessing she didn't cool you down?"

"You could say that," Preston said moving away from the window. He went to his bed and plopped down on the hard mattress. "She did look good, didn't she, John?"

"Good, hell! Man, she's hotter than a habanero pepper! Who is she?"

"Names Karen O'Day, a junior transfer from UK. She lives in Potter Hall."

"So that's why you're standing at the window, O'Day dreaming," John Wayne said laughing, and then belching loudly. "You gonna see her again?" he garbled wiping his mouth with back of his hand.

"Probably."

"What are you going to tell Mona when she finds out about this babe?"

Preston shrugged his shoulders, an uncertain look shadowing across his face. "I don't know, John. I'll cross that bridge when I come to it."

John Wayne chuckled. "I want to be there when you do."

Chapter 4

Sunday morning Mona Cooper was geared for battle drinking coffee and sitting stone straight in the far booth of the Hilltopper Restaurant. She pretended to study, but the fact nothing had been written in her notebook, and no pages in the Econ textbook had been turned betrayed her progress.

She was too upset to study, and her angry eyes darted to the front door and back to the book every few seconds. When Preston finally strolled in, she slammed the pen on the table and waited with a stiff lip. The moment he slid onto the seat he knew she'd heard about the beautiful brunette.

She closed the textbook and placed it on the seat. She picked up the coffee cup, took a sip, and then set it back on the table, all while never looking at him. After giving him several seconds of the cold treatment, she said, "I'm surprised to see you up so early."

Here we go, Preston thought as he settled on the seat opposite her. "What's that supposed to mean?" He picked up a menu, glanced at it, then tossed it aside.

"I heard about you last night."

"Yeah?"

"I heard you had a good time."

"I did."

"They said you had a very good time."

"Give me a break, Mona. What the hell did you hear?"

"I heard you had a date with a bimbo Miss Whoever last night, and that you left the party with her."

"I don't know what you're talking about. But yeah, I had a good time, but I didn't have a date. You didn't want to go with me, so I had a good time without you."

"You're an asshole."

"And you're the one who said we needed to cool things a little bit."

"Cooling it and going out with other people are two different things."

"Not in my book, Mona. But for your information I didn't 'go out' with Miss Whoever. All we did was walk outside the Fraternity house because the damn place was a smoke factory. We talked for a few minutes, and when she got cold, I drove her to Potter Hall, nothing more."

"She could have walked, it's not that far."

"Oh, for crying out loud. It was cold! Lighten up!" He picked up the menu again, tossed it aside again, then stood and went to the counter. He returned to table with a cup of coffee. "What are you studying?"

"Economics," she said coolly, "got a test Wednesday."

"I thought that was why you stayed home last night. Surely that class is not that hard."

"We all aren't Mensa candidates, Preston," she snapped. "Some of us have to work for our grades."

He sighed and pushed away from the table. "Mona, you're wearing me out, and I'm not in the mood for this shit. I'll call you later."

He looked at his watch and decided to stroll over to Potter Hall and see Karen. Potter Hall was one of the oldest dormitories on campus. Ivy crept over the old brick veneer like moss on the oak trees. Large white columns stood stately in the front, reminiscent of the grandeur of the traditional southern mansions. Hundred-year-old oak trees shaded the entrance, a magnificent picture for the eyes. Preston Desmond sauntered in the front door and approached Sue Griffin, working at the front desk.

"Good morning, Sue," he said using his famous toothy smile.

"Good morning, Preston," she answered with an inviting smile of her own displaying perfectly straight white teeth.

"Sue," I need your help," he said leaning casually against the counter. "Would you ring Karen O'Day's room for me please."

Sue's forehead narrowed as she brushed a lock of blonde hair away from her face and folded it behind her left ear with her little finger. "Who was that?" she said. Her expression puzzled him.

"Karen O'Day."

"Preston, that name doesn't sound familiar to me," she said with a slightly embarrassed smile. "But, then again, I still don't know everyone who lives here. Let me check our listings." She picked up the dormitory directory and ran her fingers over the list of names three times. She closed the book, and with an apologetic lift of her shoulders, said, "I'm sorry Preston, but Karen O'Day doesn't live here."

Preston forced a slight chuckle. "I know I had a few drinks last night, but I'd swear I brought her here about 10:30. I watched her walk in the front door."

Sue shrugged a helpless gesture. "I don't know what to tell you. You can look through the book if you'd like."

"No, no, never mind. I believe you."

He walked out of the dorm, got in the Vette, and drove aimlessly through the streets of Bowling Green. The feeling of dread, of impending doom, that the sky was falling on him and there was nothing he could do about it hit him again. He couldn't shake the feeling that had been haunting him since Saturday night. It washed over him like a water fall the moment Sue Griffin said Karen O'Day did not live in Potter Hall.

Why would she lie about something so insignificant? It didn't make sense. Not caring where he was headed, he found himself on the 31W By-Pass in front of the Town Towers motel. Impulsively, he whipped into the parking lot, and came to a stop in front of the restaurant.

He walked into the restaurant, moved to the set of doors to his right, and went into the lounge adjacent to the diner. The place was dark and quiet, with about twenty-five to thirty tables scattered across the room in no apparent order. A baby grand piano sat in the far-right corner, the bar straight ahead.

He straddled a stool at the bar and said. "Beer."

"Kind?" the heavy set red cheeked bartender said.

"Blue Ribbon…"

The bartender nodded, went to the cooler behind him, pulled out a Pabst, popped the cap, and placed it on the bar. Preston dropped a dollar on the bar, picked up the bottle and walked to the table next to the exit door near the piano.

He was halfway through the bottle when the door opened and a middle age man wearing a University of Kentucky baseball cap and denim overalls walked in and settled on the barstool at the end of the bar.

"Hello, Pete," the bartender said. "What'll it be?"

"Hey, Jake. Give me a Jim Beam, neat."

Jake poured two fingers of whiskey in a glass and placed it on the bar. Pete took a sip and then set the glass on the table, grinning like a possum eating roadkill cat guts. He took a deep breath through his nose and puffed out his chest.

"Thought I saw a movie star in the parking lot a few minutes ago."

"Oh, is that right?" Jake said with only a slight spark of interest as he wiped water from the bar.

"Yeah," Pete said. "For a minute I thought I was looking at Natalie Wood sittin' in a big Ford out front. Good lookin' woman looked just like her."

Both heads jerked toward the door when Preston dropped the bottle on the table and rushed from the room.

Once in the alley he looked both ways, then turned right toward the by-pass and ran around the building. He came to a stop next to his car scanning both sides of the street.

Damn it, she's gone!

Irritated, with her and himself, he jerked open the Vette door, looked around the parking lot one more time, then got in a drove to Sandstone Manor.

Chapter 5

Monday, he went through the motions like a dead man walking, his insides quivering like maggots feasting on a rotten corpse. In class he found himself staring out the window hoping to see Karen O'Day. Football practice was terrible. An All-American candidate who hadn't fumbled the ball in a two hundred and thirty-three carries, today he fumbled three times and dropped eight passes that were right in his hands. If that wasn't bad enough, he tripped over his own feet running untouched down the sideline. Coach Denes was not only dumb founded, he was speechless.

The library was as quiet as a cathedral at midnight, unusual for seven-thirty p.m. Preston was drawn to the place. The atmosphere in the old building never failed to motivate him. He felt at home in the hallowed surroundings. The musky smell of old books, the aged furniture, the antique artwork, it was almost sexual. He loved it, and besides, when you roomed with John Wayne McKinney you might as well forget about studying in your room. It was a madhouse. How McKinney managed to stay eligible to play football was one of life's great mysteries.

A soft hand on his shoulder sent cold shivers racing through his body, yet the warm honeyed voice melted him.

"Hi, Freddy," she said softly. "I've been waiting for you."

He turned, meeting her piercing eyes with his. For a split-second a strange unexplained panic shot through him. He smiled timorously trying to discreetly shake off the feeling.

"What did you call me?" he said.

"Why, Freddy of course," Her voice wistful sounding like filled with a sad longing. "I've always loved that name…Frederick Preston Desmond. It's a beautiful name."

In the soft lights of the library her dark eyes appeared faraway, as if she were under a spell, or in a hypnotic trance. Her unreadable eyes frightened him, yet mesmerized him, repulsed him, yet excited him. Inexplicably, and stranger still, her eyes gripped him until his heart felt a burning ache of love, deep heart-breaking love. The kind of love poets write about, the kind that never dies.

His mind screamed this is crazy, totally insane. It's impossible to be in love with a girl you just met, someone you know nothing about; someone who stabs icicles of cold fear into your guts until your gonads want to crawl up and hide inside your belly.

"Are you, okay?" She asked tracing her fingers across the back of his neck. Shock waves shot through him.

"What? Uh…yeah, I'm okay. You just caught me by surprise."

"You act like you've seen a ghost." A veiled smile tickled her lips. She quickly tightened it away. "Are you sure you're okay?"

He reached up and ran his fingers through his hair pushing it off his forehead.

"Yeah, I was just in deep thought…studying. You surprised me, that's all. No one ever calls me Freddy."

"Well, they should, it's a nice name." she paused, her eyes glaring into his appeared to harden into black stones. "You know, I've heard you're just like him. Everyone says you were born to be a very important person. That's probably why you were named after him." Her face lightened, and she chuckled, but Preston sensed the sarcasm.

"I don't know about that," he said, "In fact, I don't know very much about the man. My parents divorced when I was young. Then my dad died when I was twelve. There were a lot of hard feelings between my mother and the Desmond side of the family. I haven't seen my grandparents since Dad died."

"That is *so* sad," she said still holding his arm. "You should learn more about your roots."

She settled on the chair next to him and casually placed her left hand high on the inside of his thigh. Her pinky finger briefly rubbed his crotch and his heart rate jumped a beat. He shifted on the chair, causing her hand to slide off his leg, and turned toward her.

"Karen, why did you say you lived in Potter Hall? I went there yesterday, and they'd never heard of you. I felt like an idiot. What's going on?"

Her eyes narrowed and darted away. "I did live there for a while?" she said, and then shrugged as if to say so what. "It just kind of slipped out. After I said it, I couldn't take it back."

"Are you even a student?"

"No, not anymore."

"Did you think it would make a difference?"

"I didn't know," she said placing her hand back on his thigh and gently squeezing.

Her touch made the urge to take her in his arms nearly impossible to fight. The spell was broken when she looked at her watch. She expelled a rush of air and jerked to her feet like a puppet on a string.

"I have to go," she said tensely.

"It's only eight o'clock, you just got here!"

"I'm late, I have to go now."

"But...?"

"It's complicated, Preston. I have to go home, now!" She looked deeply into his eyes and touched his face. Her hand felt cold against his cheek.

"Look, my car is right outside," he said. "Let me take you home."

"So is mine, how do you think I got here!" The intensity of her rebuke stunned him. Her voice softened. "Not tonight," she said looking away. She paused for a moment, then said, "I'm sorry. I shouldn't have snapped at you, but I've got to be somewhere in half an hour."

"All of a sudden?"

"No, Preston. I just remembered there is something I have to do."

His eyes hooded as he nodded his head.

Her lips curled in a covert smile. "I can meet you tomorrow night in front of Cherry Hall at ten. Is that okay?"

Whatever it was in her mesmerizing gaze that made him hesitate he didn't know. Finally, he managed to say, "Yeah, if you say so."

"Don't act like that. Your grandfather wouldn't pout."

"I don't know what he would have done, and I'm not pouting. Besides, I'm not my grandfather."

"Are you sure?" She said, then chuckled softly.

"What do you mean by that?"

"Nothing, Preston. I was just teasing."

"Karen, I don't get it. At the party you made me feel...you acted like...well, I don't know, different."

"How did I make you feel different, Preston? What do you mean?"

"You made me feel like you wanted me. You knew all about me."

"I do want you, Preston. I want you very much."

Several moments of strained silence passed between them before he said, "Karen...are you married?"

A flash of anger swept across her face accompanied by a mordant chuckle. "No, Preston...I'm not married."

"Then what's the problem?"

"Listen, I guarantee you will understand everything...soon." She bent down and kissed him her lips hot, almost feverish. "Don't forget, Cherry Hall, 10 p.m."

Chapter 6

Preston Desmond leaned back in his chair, propped his feet up on the desk, and was getting ready to read the latest article in Sports Illustrated about himself when John Wayne McKinney swung open the door and stormed into the room. He unceremoniously dropped his large body on his bed and let out a deep frustrated sigh. Etched across his face a scowl that read mess with me and I'll break your spine.

Preston closed the magazine and tossed it on the desk. "What's buggin' you, brother?"

"I've got a test Tuesday and I can't find my political science book. I thought I left it in my locker in the weight room. Swore I did. Went over there to get it. I didn't. Don't know what I did with the damn thing."

"Don't worry about it. I had that class last semester, and I've still got the book. You can use it. It's over here," Preston said nodding toward the shelf over his desk.

John Wayne grinned and released a relieved sigh. "You're a life saver, my man. I could kiss you!"

"Yeah, that's me," Preston said with a chuckle, "a genuine super hero."

"Today you are. You know I'm on probation this season. I really have to pass this test." He shook his head and laughed. "With my luck the book will show up some time next semester."

He got up and went across the room, reached over Preston's shoulder, and picked the textbook off the shelf. He went back to his bunk and thumbed through the pages then stopped and snapped his finger.

"Oh yeah," he said, "before I forget. Doc Johnson wants you to call him when you get a chance."

Doc Johnson was the Athletic Director at Western. Short, squat, and balding, he looked anything but athletic. Looks are deceiving, before taking the AD job at Western Kentucky, Jerry Johnson had spent twelve years as the starting catcher for the Cincinnati Reds; three of those years he was the starting catcher for the National League in the All-Stars game. A freak auto accident injured his back, ending his playing career. After the initial depression ebbed, he went back to school and earned his Doctorate in Education. His rise to AD started when he was hired to coach the baseball team. This was his twelfth year as AD.

Preston gave a puzzled frown. "Did he say what he wanted?"

"Nope, he just said it was important, and for you to call him."

"Humph," Desmond grunted. "I wonder what that's about. I'll call him now." He rose from his chair and headed for the door. The public phone hung on the wall three rooms down the hall to the left. He dialed the athletics office, and let it ring about five times. He was starting to hang up when Doc Johnson answered.

"Hello…"

"Doc, this is Preston Desmond. John Wayne said you wanted me to call."

"Oh, hello Preston, yeah I did. You were quick."

"He said it was important."

"It's not really important. I just wanted to let you know that yesterday while we were trying to get things ready for the remodeling, we came across decades old photographs and trophies, you know, memories that accumulate through the years. Well, three of the boxes that we found are full of old pictures of your grandfather Desmond. Some good action shots, stills, group pictures, portraits, plaques, you name it. The guy was a really big man on campus." He paused for several moments before his voice took on a somber tone. "Preston, I think you really will find them interesting. If you want me to hold them, I can keep them up here for a couple of days. If not, because of the lack of space we have, we'll have to do a deep purge. Do you want to look?"

"I sure do, Doc," Preston said sounding more eager than he really was. What he felt was a feeling of relief, a reprieve from a dark guilt that he couldn't understand. He expelled a deep, silently breath, and then said, "I'm free this afternoon, Doc. How about two o'clock. I can come over then, if that works for you."

"That works for me. See you then."

Chapter 7

Preston, followed closely by John Wayne McKinney, walked into Doc Johnson's office at precisely 2:00 pm. Doc was busy working at his desk. His clothes were rumpled, and what remained of his hair stood askew. A half empty cup of black coffee next to a partially eaten donut sat in front of him. He looked up, took a sip of the coffee, and set the cup down on a folded napkin.

He greeted them with a tired smile and motioned to the two chairs in front of his desk with a flip of his wrist. He lifted the donut, took a bite, and then tossed the remaining half in the waste can, never taking his eyes off McKinney.

"I thought you had a poli-sci test to study for today, JW. What are you doing here?" he asked pointedly.

"I did study, Coach," John Wayne replied. "I'm taking a break."

"You better pass that test, son. We need you on the field, not sitting in your street clothes."

"I know it Doc. Coach Denes has a tutor working with me. I've been studying all morning."

"Um-huh, right" Johnson muttered skeptically.

"He really has been studying, Doc. No joke," Preston said. "But he was two pages away from throwing a John McKinney fit, so I figured I needed to get him away from that book and out of the dorm for a little while."

Johnson's dubious stare studied McKinney for several seconds. Then, with a deep sigh and a resigned shake of his head, said, "You know what's at stake, John." After several awkward moments he gestured toward Preston. "Come on, I'll show you guys what I'm talking about."

He led them down a narrow hall. The walls on both sides were covered with posters and photographs of great moments in Western's storied sports history. Preston Desmond's chest swelled full of self-absorbed pride knowing he was part of the Western Kentucky greats, and that someday his photo would join the collection.

He wished he could spend more time looking at them all, but Johnson was already two flights of stairs ahead. Preston hurried to catch up. At the top of the stairs Johnson led them down another hall with more pictures and into a large room filled with boxes, wooden crates and book shelves. The musky smell of old cardboard, books, and mold filled the air.

Johnson walked across the room to where three large boxes were sitting on a rectangular folding table. Each box was about the size of military footlockers.

"I put everything I thought you might be interested in, in here," he said tapping his hand on top of the first box. "I think you'll find the contents fascinating." He tapped the box again, and said, "Now, I have to get back to work. When you guys get finished, just lock the door behind you when you leave." He gave McKinney another evil eye and left the room.

"Johnson's harder on me than Coach Denes," John Wayne growled.

"He's worried about your eligibility, JW. Once you pass the test, he'll be on someone else's back."

"Yeah, I know. But busting my ass about it won't help!"

"That's true," Preston said nodding agreement, "Forget about it right now and let's see what so fascinating." He gestured with his index finger toward the box in front of McKinney. "Why don't you start lookin' in that box, and let's get this over with."

Preston grabbed the first box, slid it close, and flipped open the lid. The box was full of old photographs, certificates and plaques. He began shuffling through the pictures, glancing calmly at the strangers, and then placing the photos on the table next to the box. The plaques and certificates were briefly skimmed over, and then stacked on the floor.

He was beginning to wonder why Doc Johnson thought he'd like to see this mess when he casually reached for a picture lying face down in the pile and flipped it over. It was a picture of Frederick Desmond holding a large trophy, smiling ear to ear.

Preston had seen many pictures of his grandfather as an older man. But it just dawned on him that he'd never seen one of the young Fredrick Desmond. The image sent a shock wave rippling through him like touching a bare electric wire. It was like he was looking at himself.

"Good lord, Preston," John Wayne said holding up a hand full of glossy black and white 8x10's. "Take a look at these! Man, can you believe it? You look just like your old granddaddy!"

Preston half nodded. Although the storeroom was cold, he had to wipe off beads of sweat starting to form on his forehead.

"Yeah, I see a resemblance."

"Resemblance my ass," John Wayne shouted. "It ain't a little resemblance Pal. You look dead on like him, all the way down to that little white spot in your hair over the ear." He held out another, smaller picture. "And look at this one. It looks like you're wearing one of the old football uniforms." He returned to shuffling the pictures until he found another photograph. "Here's one that looks like you in one of those old school sweaters." He paused and shook his head. "I swear, Prez. I've never seen anything like it. This must be a joke, it's too freaking weird. If somebody asked me who's in these pictures, I'd swear on my mother's head that it's you. You're identical!"

"Yeah, it is kind of freaky," Preston mumbled staring at the stack of photos spread out over the table.

There was no doubt about it. He looked like Frederick Desmond, and it was more than a family resemblance. They looked like identical twins from the same egg only born fifty years apart. Okay, maybe you can try to explain it by saying they were family; or maybe it was just the way the camera caught the image.

Yeah, maybe, that would be strange enough, but it wasn't Grandpa Frederick that caused his stomach to flop like a fish out of water. It was the sepia toned 4x6 of the beautiful young woman with long black hair, hair that made you want to run your fingers in its luxurious beauty. A neck that made you long to nuzzle in the warm softness, breathing her intoxicating scent. A young woman whose hypnotically dark eyes seemed to pull you into their depths and grab your soul, squeezing until you screamed for mercy.

Sweat popped out on his forehead joining the bead forming over his lip. "Take a look at this, JW," he said handing the picture to John Wayne. "This girl looks like Karen, doesn't she?"

John Wayne took the picture. He pulled it up near his eyes, turned it sideways, diagonally, and upright, studying it closely, his eyes narrowing into slits, his face screwed up like someone smelling a rotten dog carcass.

"Buddy," he said handing the picture back to Preston. "Somebody's pranking you, stud. I don't know who, or why, or how, but this stuff's just too weird to be real...too damn weird to believe!"

"They look real to me, John."

"Of course, they look real. It wouldn't be a very good prank if they didn't."

"How could anybody make all this stuff up, create it, take all these pictures...any of it?" Preston said. He let out a labored breath, turned, and sat down on the table. "Tell me, John. How could they sneak in here and plant all of this without getting caught...and why?"

John Wayne rolled his eyes, his cheek muscles flexing. "I don't know, buddy. But what else could it be? You think a girl you met at a keg party who claims her name is Karen O'Day is a ghost? Come on, Preston, you're smarter than that."

John picked up a couple of the pictures and tossed them on the table in front of Preston. "Now these are the real Karen O'Day, my friend. Not some nitwit playing a stupid friggin' joke. I don't know how they did it, or why they're doing it, but somebody is trying to get in your head." He paused and slapped his palm on Preston's shoulder. "Prez, I can see why you could look so much like your grandpa; he's close blood but…"

"This girl is blood. She's Karen's aunt," Preston said. "She dated Grandpa. She was in love with him."

"So now I guess she's come back to haunt you because you look like the old man. That's some of the silliest shit I've heard in a long time. You're smarter than that… Jees…What are the odds of you and Karen O'Day looking like your ancestors. It's impossible, these pictures were planted."

Chapter 8

Julie Cramer sat at the dressing table wiping the makeup off her face. It was a beautiful face with full pouty kissable lips, a slender nose with a little knot on the bridge, and high cheek bones like that Italian movie star Sophia Loren. Her skin was flawless on a 30-year-old body that looked as though it hadn't aged a minute in the ten years since her college days on the hill. As if that wasn't enough, her most alluring feature was her eyes; dark, smoldering, slightly slanted eyes that seemed to draw you into a spider's web of desire. It was hard to break free of those hypnotic eyes.

She had a stable of regulars who would only go up the stairs with her. She heard that one of her johns had told Pauline that once you'd had sex with Julie, screwing any of other girls would be like going from lobster to catfish, and lobster smelled better. The memory made her chuckle.

Several of her regulars thought she was a coed. She never said whether she was, or she wasn't. If they wanted to believe they were having sex with a college girl, then let them. Of course, she wasn't. That was something Pauline would never allow. The policy was no college girls, period. If anything could bring down the wrath of the citizens of Warren County, it would be that she was employing college girls in her brothel.

She'd been working at the house on Clay Street for a little more than a month when she first learned that Frederick Preston Desmond had returned to the hill. The news that he was here, that he had come back to the scenes of his crimes, hit her like double mule kicks to the gut. Every time she saw his picture, or heard his name on the radio, she would grab the book from her dresser, look at the pictures of Karen O'Day hanging from the bridge, and her hatred would boil to the edge. Something had to be done!

Then one night in the middle of a tryst the seeds of revenge began to grow. The seeds of the way to bring justice to Karen O'Day…to bring justice to her, for anyone with half a brain could see that she was really Karen…Karen O'Day. But Pauline liked to rotate the girls in the syndicate, and it wouldn't be long before she was moved away from the city of Bowling Green. Time was running out.

Staring somberly at the reflection looking back at her she gently rubbed the remaining makeup off her face and tossed the Kleenex in the wastepaper can. she splashed a minute amount of Lilac and Roses perfume in her palm and rubbed the oily fragrance on her neck breathing in the delicious bouquet. Finally, she reached up and unpinned the red wig from her head and placed it on the head mannequin. She moved the mannequin to her dresser and with a crooked smile removed the hair pins holding up her black hair. She smiled at herself in the mirror as she shook her head and watched the beautiful raven locks cascade down over her shoulders.

I'm coming for you, Freddy! she thought. *Lord, I'm tired, thank God the milk can is in the driveway.*

The johns knew whenever the milk can was in the middle of the driveway Pauline's was closed.

Chapter 9

"I'm sorry, Preston," the registrar Janice Martin said. The slender middle-aged woman pushed her eyeglasses up on the top of her head revealing surprisingly bright blue eyes. "We don't keep records that old at this location. They're all stored in a warehouse down on Clay Street. Why in the world would you want to go through all those old records?"

"I'm doing a research paper for one of my classes," he lied. "My assignment is to try and trace down some of the old grads from the class of 1920. You know, to see how their lives turned out."

She smiled. "Now that's something I believe would be interesting to read. But it sounds like a whole lot of work."

"Yes ma'am. I'm finding that out," he said, "but thanks anyway. I'll figure something out."

He chuckled and gave her his best Preston Desmond smile. He started to turn toward the door when she touched his arm.

"Hold on a minute, Preston. I know another place you might want to try. The library has all the old year books. If I'm not mistaken, they list the student's hometown. That might give you a place to start." She hesitated and then added, "The only other person I know who may be able to help you is a lady named Maude Semonian."

"Who's Maude Semonian?"

"She was the librarian here for several years. I believe she graduated from Western around that time. She still lives in Bowling Green."

"That sounds great Mrs. Martin. Thanks."

Preston hurried out of the Registrar's office and headed to the library. The index cards led him to a section on the top floor that was dedicated to the history of the college, and to the city of Bowling Green. He located the yearbooks and began searching for the year 1920. He found it on the top shelf. He pulled it from the shelf and walked to the study table located in the middle of the room and sat down.

The yearbook looked new, without a mark in it. He flipped it open and quickly thumbed through the pages. He was sure Karen O'Day was either in the Junior or Senior class, but just to be sure he didn't miss anything, he scoured through each grade level.

He was starting to think maybe JW was right. Maybe someone was playing a joke on him. He started to laugh. The chuckle froze on page 48: Napier, Newton, O'Bannon, O'Connell, O'Day…Karen O'Day!

A knot harder than a golf ball formed in his throat. What the hell is going on? The picture over the name was identical to the girl who knew so much about him. The beautiful girl who knew even more about his grandfather than he did. How?

Coincidence? He hurriedly flipped through the pages until he reached the sports section. Rapidly turning to the pictures of the cheerleaders. He slammed the book shut. A sick feeling like swallowing a lump of cold grease hit the pit of his stomach.

Feeling confused he fell back in the chair, his mind swirling. The whole thing was nuts. He'd touched her. She was warm flesh and blood, not a figment of his imagination, not a spirit or a ghost, or whatever you wanted to call it.

Shaken, he went back into the stacks and slid the book back in its place.

Determined to get to the bottom of the mystery, he reached in his pocket and pulled out the piece of paper that the Registrar had written Maude Semonian's telephone number on. He ran down the steps to the main floor and went to the row of telephones on the wall in the hall.

He called Maude Semonian, and then for moral support called Mona Cooper.

Chapter 10

"Give me one reason why I should help you find out anything about this, quote, fascinating, unquote, woman you met at a drunken fraternity party," Mona Cooper said sharply as she opened the Corvette door and slid onto the seat. Her face looked as red as the turtleneck sweater she was wearing. She sighed angrily and flattened her skirt with both hands, staring straight ahead. The very thought of helping him was infuriating. "The last I heard we were getting ready to announce our engagement, and now you want to find out everything you can about this strange woman."

"We are going to get married, Mona," Preston said feeling like a fool. "I love you, believe me. But since I met her…I don't know, I can't explain it. It's like I'm under a spell. It's like I've been drugged…I can't stop thinking about her."

"Are you completely out of your mind, Preston? What are you thinking?" she snapped, then pause and took a breath. "Are you on drugs? I know you sprained your back last week. Did the doctor give you something that's making you act this way? Is that it? Because that's a hell of a thing to say to the woman you're going to marry!"

Preston nodded helplessly. "I know it sounds crazy, Mona. But…but… I don't know…it's like I'm obsessed."

"Oh my God, that is the biggest crock…"

Before she could explode, he quickly said, "I know it sounds crazy, and I can't explain it, but I swear it's the truth. JW saw the pictures of Grandpa Desmond and Karen O'Day. You can ask him, Mona. The girl I met at the party looks exactly like the girl in the pictures. She even has the same name"

"No, that's what she calls herself," Mona said.

He sat quietly staring at the dashboard. After several minutes he turned toward her and cupped her hand in his. "You're right, babe. I'm acting stupid. That's why I want you with me when I talk to Maude Semonian."

Mona lifted her gaze until her hooded eyes met his, her lips pressed tight. "Preston, I'm going to do this just for you. But I swear, if you leave me for this woman, I'll…I'll fix your wagon."

"You don't have to worry about that," he said. He fired up the Corvette, and drove out of the dormitory parking lot, turned right on College Heights Blvd., then made a left on State Street. He located the address Mrs. Semonian had given him and pulled next to the curb in front of a neat two-story white clapboard house. He got out, went around and opened the door for Mona, and followed her up the weather cracked sidewalk to Maude's front door.

Maude Semonian met them at the door with a friendly smile. She looked several years older than sixty-seven, the lines crisscrossing her face like a city road map, her back twisted and stooped with arthritis, each step looked painful. Life was taking a heavy toll. Still, the cheerfulness she projected contradicted the grouse that Mrs. Martin at the registrar's office implied.

She led them into a spotless, well-kept living room, full of lively colors, exotic paintings on the walls, and several varieties of potted plants. After they were seated, she went to the kitchen, and returned a few minutes later with a carafe of coffee and three cups. Preston was amazed at the steady hand lifting the offered cups. His hand shook more that hers.

"Lord, boy," she said with a hoarse chuckle. "When I opened the door and saw you standing there, I thought I'd died and gone to heaven." she dabbed a napkin to her thin lips and nodded her head rhythmically.

"Why is that, Mrs. Semonian?" He asked smiling mechanically.

"Please call me Maude, Preston."

"Okay…ma'am. Why did you think you had died?"

"Because honey, for a second there I thought Freddy Desmond was standing at my door!" She wrinkled her thinning brow. "Did anyone ever tell you that you look exactly like your grandfather?"

"I've heard there was a resemblance," he said.

"A resemblance my arthritic foot," she scoffed. She pushed to her feet slowly and scuffled stiffly to the bookcase that lined all four walls of the den. She stepped up on a stool and slowly ran a twisted finger across the backs of several volumes. "Ah yes, here it is."

She pulled a large leather-bound hardback book from the shelf and turned around holding the volume forward.

"I'm proud of this work," she said. She went back to the couch and seated herself between Preston and Mona. "I co-wrote it with Robert Jones. Professor Jones had his personal demons, but he was a great historian." She moved the book around so Mona could see her name printed at the bottom of the cover. "It's a history of the city of Bowling Green. Naturally the college is a big part of what's in the book since it's such a big part of the town."

Mona nodded and smiled sweetly. "I'm sure it was a lot of work."

"It was a labor of love, my dear," Maude replied, "a labor of love." She shifted her attention from Mona to Preston and opened the book. "Tell me, Preston. How much do you know about your grandfather?"

"Not very much I'm afraid. The only thing I know about him is that he was a United States Senator for twelve years, that he was very rich, and that he died in office." He paused, took a sip of the coffee, and then placed the cup back on the table. "When my parents divorced, I was too young to know what was going on. My grandmother on dad's side hated my mother. The feeling was mutual. Mother never talked about Dad or the Desmond's. I've never heard anything about his early years."

"That's a shame," Maude said with a tsk-tsk of the tongue and a sympathetic shake of her head. "Family warfare always hurts the innocent." She breathed a deep sigh and continued. "Well, let me try to remember what I know about Freddy."

She stopped for a moment, her milky eyes clouding over as long-buried memories brought a gentle smile to her dry cracked lips. The fingers of her right hand unconsciously toyed with the collar of her blouse.

"Freddy Desmond was gorgeous. All the young women on campus were after him." She smiled a knowing smile at Mona. "I suspect you have the same problem, don't you dear. I'm sure girls chase Preston."

"You wouldn't believe how aggressive some girls can be," Mona said her face revealing the insecurity his popularity caused.

Maude reached over, patted Mona's knee, and squeezed gently. "I'm sure you have nothing to worry about, my dear. He loves you it's written all over him." She smiled sweetly, and then turned her attention back to the book. She flipped past several pages to the index and then ran a finger down the page.

"You know, it's absolutely scary how much you really do look like your grandfather, Preston. It's almost as if you're the same person." Maude chuckled and wrinkled her nose apologetically. "I'm getting a little off track, aren't I. You called about Karen O'Day, didn't you?"

"Yes ma'am," Preston replied, the hair on his arms crawling from the comparison with his grandfather.

"I think the whole idea of Preston looking so much like his grandpa has him a little paranoid," Mona said. "Especially since he met a girl at an Alpha Tau Epsilon party Saturday who said her name is Karen O'Day."

Maude's thin lips tightened, her back went ramrod straight. She reached down, picked up her coffee cup and sipped quietly for a full minute. Finally, she breathed deeply through her nose, looked at Preston, and said, "This girl said her name is Karen O'Day?"

"Yes," Mona answered for him.

Maude grunted. "That is really interesting. It's also mighty coincidental!"

"What do you mean?" Preston asked.

"Your grandfather met Karen O'Day at a Duke's party. Since you're an A.T.E. member, Preston, I'm sure you already know that the Dukes were the forerunners of Alpha Tau Epsilon. Although there were no fraternities in those days, we still had our social clubs that partied and hung out together."

She smiled as the years flashed back into her mind. "From that night on," she said, "Freddy and Karen were practically inseparable. They were madly in love. It was a fairytale come to life; the rich handsome football star, and the beautiful cheerleader from the poor side of town. God she was envied!" Maude leaned back on the sofa and rested her liver spotted hands on top of the *City of Bowling Green* history book and looked at Preston. "Karen probably would have been your grandmother if it hadn't happened."

"If what hadn't happened?" Preston asked.

Maude's smile morphed into an unhappy grimace as she looked down and began searching through the pages of the book. When she located what she wanted, she stopped and turned the book so both Mona and Preston could see the grainy photo of a young woman hanging from a covered bridge. The caption in fine print said the photo was courtesy of the Bowling Green Police archives.

"This is what happened to Karen O'Day," she said quietly, almost reverently.

"She committed suicide?" Mona asked leaning against Maude's shoulder to get a better look at the picture.

"Oh no, dear!" Maude said shaking her head vigorously, "Karen didn't commit suicide. She was murdered."

"Damn..." Preston whispered as another snake of anxiety began slithering inside his chest. "Did they catch the killer?"

"Oh my, yes," Maude said. "The police were very good. They arrested him three hours after Karen's body was discovered. Not only was everyone amazed about how fast they caught him, but it surprised us all because of who did it."

"You knew the killer?" Preston asked. "It wasn't a stranger?"

"Yes, we knew him very well," she sighed. "He was a teammate of Freddy's named Felix Curtis. When they arrested him, he was lying on his bunk in the dorm, studying, calm as could be."

She looked down at the book and flipped through the pages until she came to several pictures documenting the murder, the capture, and the subsequent trial. "I've always thought it strange that he never tried to run away," she said staring straight ahead, a faraway look in her eyes.

Curiously, the look on her face sent another hot wave of angst flushing over him. *What the hell is wrong with me?* He shook off the feeling, and said, "Did Felix Curtis ever say why he killed her?"

"Oh no, he never did," Maude said shaking her head. "Felix claimed he was innocent up to the very last minute. According to witnesses at the execution his last words were 'my Lord Jesus knows I am an innocent man.'

"His attorneys tried to get the conviction overturned, but all of the appeals were denied. The courts said that although the evidence was circumstantial it was enough for a reasonable jury to convict. He was hanged three months after he was convicted."

"Good Lord, he was executed that quickly?" Mona exclaimed. "The evidence must have been overwhelming."

"Not really," Maude answered. "Things were a lot different in those days. Judges didn't mess around like they do today. A condemned man had one or two appeals. If they were denied, then in most cases that was it."

Mona bit her lip and shook her head. She hated the death penalty, and it sounded to her like Felix Curtis didn't stand a chance. "What possible evidence did they have that could justified the State of Kentucky killing him?" Mona muttered tersely.

Maude's brow wrinkled at the tone. "Well, my dear, there were two pieces that nailed his coffin so to speak. One, his student identification card was found lying in the mud just a few feet from where Karen was hanging. The other was a small shred of material found stuck under Karen's fingernail. It matched a shirt the police found in Felix Curtis' closet. The pocket had been torn off. Curtis swore up and down that the shirt wasn't his, that he had never seen the shirt before. His closest friends testified they had never seen him wear it."

"And he was hanged based on that?" Preston said incredibly. "I doubt if he would even be convicted today."

Maude shrugged. "Maybe, maybe not, who knows. I know I was certainly convinced that he killed her." She picked up her coffee cup, took a small sip, and set the cup down. "There were other things," she said with a tired sigh, "but of course they were just as sketchy. Still, with so many bits and pieces piling up they led to a guilty verdict." She shrugged again and closed the book.

"You have to remember the times, and who it was Felix killed. People in Kentucky were as outraged about the killing of Karen O'Day, as they were a decade later when the Lindbergh baby was murdered. In 1920, she was the girlfriend of the most popular athlete the state of Kentucky had ever produced. He was idolized. It was crazy, and as far as the folks sitting on the jury were concerned it was an open and shut case. Freddy Desmond deserved justice, and they were going to give it to him."

She stopped, and with a painful grimace slowly turned. "Tell me, Preston. What brought on this sudden interest in Karen O'Day?"

Feeling foolish he looked to Mona for a sign of moral support. She returned his visual pleading with a noncommittal raise of an eyebrow. Seeing that Mona was no help he decided to tell the whole story, leaving out the planned rendezvous at Cherry Hall. After he finished Maude stood up and without a word left the room. She came back a few minutes later with a fresh pot of coffee and a bottle of rye whiskey.

"After a story like that," she said with a nervous chuckle, "I think I could use a little tonic." She offered the bottle around, and when they both shook their heads, she topped off her cup, and placed the bottle on the table next to the carafe. "That was quite a story, son, but you don't really believe in the supernatural, do you?"

"I don't know what I believe anymore."

***

Four houses down State Street the occupant of a blue 1960 Ford sat in the dark watching Maude Semonian's house.

Chapter 11

Preston Desmond stood in the shadows of President Cherry's statue, his eyes scanning the campus. From this vantage point he could observe almost everything moving on the hill. Distracted for a split second by a dog running through the trees behind him he looked away. When he turned back to the statue, she was sitting on the steps in front of Cherry Hall. She looked even more beautiful than before, calmly waiting, legs crossed at the ankle, hands folded primly in her lap. He glanced at his watch, his heart racing like a nervous bride groom in front of a preacher.

It was precisely ten o'clock.

He stood watching in the dark for several minutes fighting the urge to run away. But he couldn't move. Every part of his brain told him get out now, go, never look back, but his body kept needing to be with her. To know her. He felt as if he was being pulled by a force beyond his control. The longer he stood spying on her the stronger the force grew.

Sitting on the steps, her expression never changed. Finally, he took a nervous breath and stepped into the light of the streetlamps. Hesitantly, he moved toward her.

She looked up as he approached, her lips curling in a self-assured smile.

"I almost didn't come," he said.

"I knew you would." She took his hand in both of hers and placed it against her cheek. Her hands felt as cold as a morticians table, but her face was warm. In the brisk October night, the difference made him recoil from her touch. Her piercing brown eyes darkened as she straightened her shoulders and folded her hands on her lap. "What's wrong, Preston. Have I done something to upset you?"

He side-stepped around her knees and sat down a few inches away from her, afraid if he even touched her, he would lose his nerve. He inched further away and leaned forward resting his elbows on his knees. He sat quietly wondering if she would think he was crazy. He shrugged slightly. *Oh, what the hell!*

"Karen, this morning I went to the A.D.'s office. Doc Johnson wanted me to go through several boxes of old photographs before the athletic department started throwing stuff away. Some of the pictures were taken in 1920. A lot of them were of my grandfather." He paused with a bewildered shake of his head.

"It stunned me how much we looked alike." He paused to see her reaction, but her composed gaze never wavered. "The thing that shook me the most were five pictures of him standing next to a young woman. She was beautiful, Karen. She looked exactly like you."

Karen smiled at the unintended compliment. "Okay," she said. Then with a nonchalant shrug she asked, "What are you getting at?"

"This afternoon I went to see a woman who went to school with Grandpa. She told me the girl in the picture was Grandpa Desmond's girlfriend. Her name was Karen O'Day."

"Preston," Karen said, a frown creasing her forehead. "I've already told you my aunt went to school here. I also told you she was in love with Freddy Desmond." She rose to her feet facing him, her arms stretched forward, palms up. "Yes, her name was Karen, and yes, we do look alike. But what's the problem? You, look like your grandfather, I resemble my Aunt."

"The image was exact, Karen, not a resemblance."

"Old photographs."

"My roommate said someone's pulling a joke on me. He said the pictures are doctored; they can't be real."

"Your friend is wrong, Preston. The pictures are not doctored, and no one is trying to fool you."

"Then who are you, Karen?"

There was a long silence as she paced back and forth in front of the building. After several minutes she expelled a deep exhausted sigh and closed her eyes, touching her fingers to her temples. She massaged gently for several moments, and then hung her head as if in prayer. After another long silence she nervously bit at her lower lip and whispered, "You wouldn't believe me if I told you."

"Try me!"

Another big sigh. "Very well," she said matter-of-factly. "Preston, I believe in your heart you know who I am."

"I'm not in the mood for riddles."

"It's not a riddle." A pause. "The Karen O'Day you saw in the pictures."

"Yeah?"

"It was me."

"Bullshit!"

She stood quietly watching him. "You think I'm crazy, don't you?"

"That's impossible!"

Without replying, she held out her hand. "Come with me, I want to show you something."

"What?"

"You'll see."

Feeling unable to resist he placed his hand in hers. She squeezed firmly and led him around the side of Cherry Hall, then down the wooded path to the rear of the building. Preston tried to pull his hand free, but she tightened her grip.

He was shocked at her strength. She led him further down the path to the center of campus. The way was blocked by a contractor's plywood barricade. He looked around. They were standing near the front of the old football stadium.

"Where are we going?" he said. After the remark she made about being the Karen O'Day in the pictures this walk in the dark was feeling more and more like a bad idea.

"You'll see."

"Why?"

"Because, I love you."

"You just met me."

"Um huh..."

She led him through an opening in the barricade, and once inside it was so dark, he could barely make out the concrete ruins lying all around. Then, in the dark, he felt her hands caress his face.

"Wait a minute, what's going on?"

"Shoo, don't talk," she said breathlessly. "Freddy, I've waited for you for so long."

He grabbed both her wrist and pushed her arms down. She was strong, much stronger than he expected. In the dark he could feel her body tightening. It took all he's strength to keep his grip.

"Karen, what are you doing? What are you talking about? What do you mean you've waited so long, so long for what?"

"For you, Freddy!" She screamed, her voice reaching the hysterical. "For you! I've been waiting for you far too long. But at last, the time is right. Don't you remember? Don't you know where we are?"

"Of course, this is where they're building the new library."

"No...no, no, no, no, no.... This is where you ran your touchdowns, Freddy. This is where people would cheer for you and scream for you. This is where I would cheer for you..."

"Karen, stop this! I am *not* Freddy Desmond! You're not your Aunt Karen. It is not me, and it's not you."

The anger in his voice was palpable, but she went on ignoring his denials. "...and then, after the games we would come here together."

Her right hand released its grip, and she began unbuttoning his shirt.

"Karen, stop this...come on now..."

"...and you would lay me down on this very spot..."

Her body pressed against him, her breath sweet, her fragrance intoxicating. She kissed his neck, whispering his name. Then hungrily, long pent-up passions released, she moved up to his face, her lips hot and demanding. In the blink of an eye he was on his back, and she was on top of him.

"Karen..."

"In the shadows..." she sighed.

"Don't, I'm..."

"...and you would love me...and." Her burning lips, savage and hungry, found his again and again, pressing him against the ground. The heat raging inside her, pushing on top of him, was more than his resistance could bear. And then, as if reliving a dream, he surrendered to the drug of her scent, the opiates of primal desire. They made love on the ground. It felt like déjà vu.

Afterwards, Karen lay awake until she was sure Preston Desmond was asleep. When his breath became rhythmic, she eased away from him, and silently tiptoed out between the openings in the plywood barricade. She stopped just a few yards into a group of trees near the construction site and stepped behind a tree.

She took a deep breath and rotated her shoulders to straighten the kinks out of her back caused by the hard ground. She flattened the wrinkles in her clothes with both hands and brushed the dirt away as best she could.

Pleased with herself, she glanced back to where Preston lay, grunted sarcastically, and then hurried down the hill, pausing and looking back several times. Satisfied no one was following she went on down the hill to where her car was parked on College Street. She had left it in front of the A.T.E. fraternity house as a personal private joke.

She looked around carefully one more time, then got in the Ford and headed toward town.

Chapter 12

The morning sun stirred Preston awake. He rolled over on the cardboard pallet where they made love. She was gone. Still feeling exhausted he pushed to a cross-leg sitting position, rubbed the sleep from his eyes, and glanced at his watch. It was only six-thirty. Thank God, few people would be out on campus at this hour. He stuck his head through the opening in the barricade. Seeing no one, he ran down the hill to Sandstone Manor.

John Wayne was at his desk rifling through a stack of paper when Preston pushed open the door, staggered in, and plopped exhausted on his bed.

"Where you been, Hoss?" JW asked pushing the paper aside.

"With Karen O'Day," he said.

"You were with her all night?"

"Yes, Father McKinney, I was with her all night."

McKinney tossed his pencil on the desk and swiveled around in his chair facing his roommate.

"Coach Denes made bed checks last night. He asked where you were, and I told him you were at the library. He reminded me in no uncertain terms the library was closed."

"We don't have a game this week. Why was he making bed checks?"

"How do I know, he's the coach."

"You didn't have to tell him anything. You're not your brother's keeper, and I'm not your brother."

"I was just tryin' to cover your ass, Hoss. Next time I won't."

"Fine." Preston shrugged one *who cares* shoulder and kicked off his shoes. He clasped his hands behind his head, closed his eyes, and repeated over-and-over again in his mind that it wasn't his fault. He couldn't stop himself; he was emotionally drugged. That's it, he was emotionally drugged. Karen O'Day had bewitched him, forcing him against his will.

That's ridiculous, he thought. He cheated on Mona, okay, that was wrong, maybe even unforgivable; but the simple fact of the matter is he's a man, and Karen O'Day's a very beautiful woman. A woman like none he'd ever known. And no matter how he tried to fight it, he couldn't get her out of his head.

"All I sayin' Preston, is you better talk to Coach. He wasn't very happy when he left."

"Screw coach, I'll see him at practice."

"Okay, Pal," John Wayne replied with a disgusted nod. "It's your funeral." He grunted a silent obscenity, shook his head, and turned back to his books.

The rest of the day seemed like an endless freefall of meaningless dribble, like wading through a pit of quicksand. His appetite was gone, and he stumbled through the hours like the walking dead. Karen had vanished, and the longer she stayed away the more obsessed he became. He saw her in the faces of every group of students walking across campus. He saw her sitting on a park bench in the town square, only to find when he approached it wasn't her. Karen O'Day was driving him crazy. He felt like she had cast a spell on him. A spell only she could remove.

Coach Denes was the first to see the deterioration in his star running back. The silly mistakes, the missed assignments, the wrong patterns, fights with teammates, the type of transgressions a player of his caliber would never make. In the four years Coach had known Preston the one thing that impressed him was how focused, how disciplined, the young athlete was. But now, in just a matter of a few days it seemed his desire to play was gone. It appeared he no longer cared.

In the beginning Denes tried coaxing the problem out of Preston. He went out of his way offering encouragement. He talked positive about the good play on the field. He bit his tongue when silly mistakes were made. Nothing worked, and it soon became obvious Preston's problems had nothing to do with football. That's when he summoned him to his office.

Denes was sitting on a brown leather swivel chair, drawing x's and o's on a note pad, when Preston tapped on the door. He placed the pencil on the desk, and motioned Preston in with a nod of his head. He leaned forward resting his elbows on the desk and sat staring at Preston for what seemed like a long while.

Finally, he said, "What's going on with you, Son?" Concern creased his forehead.

"Nothing, Coach," Preston mumbled lifting one shoulder in an impenetrable shrug. He slouched back in the chair sullenly.

"You sick?"

"No."

"Problems with classes?"

"Nope…"

"Girl trouble?"

"No, I'm good, I'm fine! Everything is fine."

"Well you sure don't play like everything is fine."

"Look, Coach, I'm in a slump. Everybody has a slump now and then."

Denes leaned back in his chair, his fingers creating a pyramid as he studied Preston's face. It worried him. The young man's skin looked pale and drawn. His eyes looked dark and empty, almost frightening.

Denes shook his head sadly. "Preston, are you…do you have a problem with drugs?"

Preston grunted sourly. "No, coach, I'm not using drugs. But that might be just what I need." He scooted the chair back and stood up. "Now, if that's all you wanted, I've got things I need to figure out on my own. You can't help me. Nobody can.

"I'll play football for you. I'll play the way you want me too, but in the meantime, why don't you mind your own business and leave me alone."

Chapter 13

Preston jumped out of bed, threw on yesterday's clothes, smelled his armpits, and headed straight to the library. It was a good bet they would have Maude Semonian's book. He checked the library card catalog file, located the number, and went to the history section. The only copy on the shelf looked like it had never been opened. He grinned and slid the small book by Dr. Robert P. Jones and Maude Semonian from the shelf.

He found a seat at a table near the window, and like a man possessed flipped to the appendix. He located the section that included Karen O'Day's murder. He had no idea what he was searching for, but an inner voice told him to keep looking, he would know it when he saw it.

Two hours later the search was over, and the realization sent chills crawling up his spine like a parade of spiders. Karen O'Day was murdered forty-five years ago this coming Saturday, October 16th. He couldn't understand why this was important, but the uneasy feeling gripping knots in his stomach told him it was behind everything.

He read, and then reread, the article describing how Karen O'Day was killed. The condition she was in when the two boys found her was sickening, and he felt a headache start to throb. He massaged his temples for several moments and then closed the book. He placed the volume back on the shelf and stood in the stacks waiting for the headache to ease before heading to the pay telephone in the lobby. The anxiety returned when Maude Semonian answered her phone.

"Hello," she said weakly.

"Good morning, Mrs. Semonian. I hope I didn't wake you; this is Preston Desmond."

"Why, hello, Preston. No, you didn't wake me. I've been up for a while now. How are you this morning?"

I really don't know, he thought, but said, "I'm fine ma'am I just need your help."

"How can I help you, Preston? If it's about Karen O'Day, I've already told you everything I can remember. That was a long time ago, you know."

"Yes, ma'am," he said, "It's nothing about her. Well, not exactly about her. It's that I want, no, I need to go to the covered bridge." There was silence at the other end of the line that seemed like minutes.

"What do you think you'll find there, Preston?" she asked quietly.

"I don't expect to find anything, ma'am. I just want to see the place. I need to go to the spot where it happened, and I thought maybe you could tell me how to get there."

"I'm sure there are hundreds of people in this town who could tell you how to get there."

Preston sensed a hesitation in Maude. "Is there a reason you would rather not tell me?" he asked quietly.

She coughed hoarsely, and when she spoke her voice sounded weak and tired.

"Preston," she said. "seeing you the other day, and how much you look like Freddy, brought back so many forgotten memories, it's hard to explain." She paused. "You see, Freddy and Karen were my dear friends. Her death hit me extremely hard. To say it was traumatic is an understatement..."

"Mrs. Semonian, I'm sorry, I didn't..."

"Don't be. None of this is your fault. It's just that when I saw you, I saw Freddy. And even though he was Karen's guy, I loved him. Always have, and, even though he's long since passed, I always will." She paused, and Preston thought he heard ice cubes tinkling in a glass. She sighed and continued as if far away.

"Back then, we were so young, so happy. The First World War was over, life was new, and everyone had marvelous plans for saving the world. Freddy tried his best when he was a senator, but one man can't do it alone." The ice cubes rattled again, and then she continued. "The thought that something as bad as what happened to Karen could ever happen to one of us was unimaginable. Those sorts of things only happen to other people. None of us had ever experienced the loss of someone so close, someone we cared so deeply about.

"An accident would have been bad enough," Maude continued, "but to lose one of your friends to a vicious heartless murderer was beyond comprehension."

"Mrs. Semonian, I don't mean to keep bringing up bad memories. I'll find the directions somewhere else."

"Don't be silly, I'm over the shock now. Do you have a pencil?"

"Yes, Ma'am, go ahead."

"Okay, take the 31W Bypass until you come to Scottsville Road. Go east. I don't remember how far you go before Scottsville Road become Franklin Road, but it will. Once you are on Franklin Road, I think you'll drive about ten miles..."

"Ten miles," he interjected.

"That's right," she said. "Now after you've driven, like I say, about ten miles give or take a couple, there's a small cemetery on the right; I guess it's still there. It's very small so you'll have to watch closely. When you see the cemetery, look to your left. You should see a narrow road, it's not much wider than a wagon trail. That's the old Covered Bridge Road." She stopped and coughed, and once again Preston thought he heard ice in a glass. Tonic time.

After a couple of sips Maude resumed, "The best I can remember is that the Covered Bridge Road is as crooked as a snake's path. It starts out fairly level, and then drops off real steep." Her words were broken by a shallow wheezy breath, then continued. "Once you reach the bridge, you'll find yourself nearly surrounded by cliffs. The only relief is the water in front of you. At least I guess there's still water there. It may be dry now." She was quiet for several heartbeats, then said, "Have you got it?"

"Yes, ma'am."

"You know, Preston. Karen was killed forty-five years ago."

"I know."

"That bridge was old then. It might not even exist anymore."

"I know. You're probably right Maude. I don't expect anything. I'm just curious to see where it all took place."

"Humph," Maude said, "you know what curiosity did to the cat."

"My mother used to say that all the time."

"Your mother was right. You be careful, son."

Chapter 14

The blue Ford came to a stop at the rear corner of the Sandstone Manor parking lot. Julie Cramer adjusted the seat as far back as it would go and removed the Karen O'Day murder book from the glove compartment. She knew Preston Desmond was in the building because she saw Mona Cooper go in the boarding house and she hadn't come out. She glanced at the entrance to the boarding house and opened the book. After reading the paperback so many times she could almost recite it verbatim. Each time she read it; it made her crazy.

Now, outside the bastard's home, she pictured killing him the same way he killed Karen in 1920. The thought sent a warm rush thrilling between her legs. She placed the book on the seat, reached down, and a massaged herself roughly through her panties closing her eyes as her body shuddered. She released a low gasping moan and then sat trembling for several moments. Feeling spent, she took a couple of deep breaths, picked up the book, and read the title, *The Murder of Karen O'Day*.

She closed her eyes, visualizing Preston Desmond swinging from the bridge, his face blackish blue, his tongue bulging between his brutalized lips like a putrid piece of blood pudding. In her room she had *The History of the City of Bowling Green*, and *The Murder of Karen O'Day*, both written by Dr. Robert Jones, but the difference between the two tomes was puzzling. The History strictly reported the conviction of Felix Curtis, a man with no motive or real connection to the victim, while the Murder book, written a few years later, asserted that Frederick Desmond was the killer.

Dr. Jones alleged the Desmond family's wealth, and Frederick Desmond's popularity was his get out of jail free card, only in this case a get away with murder card. The fact that the autopsy revealed Karen O'Day was pregnant was disallowed in the trial. Curtis' attorneys declared they could have used it to create reasonable doubt.

Julie Cramer tilted the book sideways and it automatically opened to Karen O'Day hanging from the bridge. Suddenly streams of sweat began running down her face, the muscles in her neck constricting, tightening as if being stretched. She cried out in pain grabbing at her throat. It felt as if her head was being pulled from her body.

Vomit filled her mouth, seeping out of the corners, and running down her chin. She grabbed frantically for the door handle and missed. Clamping her jaws together to keep the bile from spewing out in her car, she held one hand over her mouth, and felt for the handle with the other, connecting on the second try. She yanked the door open, leaned sideways out of the car, and puked on the road.

Hate burning her eyes, she pulled a tissue from her purse and wiped her mouth. She threw the wet tissue on the asphalt, fired up the engine, and drove slowly out of the parking lot, heading toward town.

Chapter 15

Julie pulled into Pauline's parking lot, locked the car, and casually walked in the back door of the brothel. Pauline was waiting next to the hall stairway, her heavy arms folded under her ample bosom, a humorless expression in her grandmotherly eyes.

"Where have you been?" Pauline asked smiling sweetly. "You've been gone all day without a word." The 'would you like a piece of pie' look on her face veiled the anger bubbling inside.

Julie shrugged impertinently. "I had personal business to take care of." She went to move around the older woman, but Pauline blocked her path. "*Excuse me*," Julie challenged, cocking her head like an insolent teenager.

"What kind of personal business did you have?" Pauline demanded.

"Personal! That kind!" Julie replied sharply. She turned sideways and edged around Pauline moving toward the stairway.

"Julie, stop right now!"

Julie froze on the first step.

"This is the fifth time in the past two weeks you were supposed to be working, but you weren't here…I was worried about you."

"Yeah, I'm sure."

Pauline's eyelids hooded. "Nobody knew where you were," she said.

"I didn't know I was on a leash."

"Don't get smart with me. You work for *me*. If you don't like the way I run this house, you're more than welcome to pack your bags and move on." She paused, studying Julie's reaction. When the young woman met Pauline's glare with eyes as blank as the morning's receipts, Pauline said, "You cost me money today. Three men came in wanting to spend time with you."

"Five other girls were working."

"They wanted you. When they found out you weren't available, they turned around and left. That cost me money. I don't like losing money! The money I don't make today is money I'll never make. You may not care about losing money, but I do."

Julie stared at the floor for a full minute without speaking. *It's not time to cut the ties,* she thought. Then, with a bitter tight smile, she swallowed hard and nodded. "You're right, Pauline. I was wrong, I apologize. I should have been here." Her lips curled into an exaggerated smile as she turned to go up the steps. Midway up she paused, grabbed the handrail, and looked back over her shoulder, her black eyes zeroing crosshairs in on Pauline. "Don't ever call me Julie Cramer again. From now on I'm using my real name…Karen O'Day."

The flash of a memory forty-five years gone hit Pauline like putrid pork, taking her back to October 1920. She was 15 years old, and there was another girl named Karen O'Day.

She was sitting on the back porch reading the August 1920 edition of *Motion Picture* magazine, when news of the murder was broadcasted over the radio. She remembered like it was yesterday how the newscaster went into vivid detail, describing how Karen O'Day died, and the terrible condition her body was in when two young boys found her.

A few months later the same newscaster described, in audibly excited tones, how people traveled hundreds of miles to see the execution of the man who killed her. Executions were public in those days, and people would go and have a picnic while waiting for the show. It was a carnival time. It was a terrible time. It was a time you never forget.

Why would Julie use Karen O'Day's name? How could she even know about the poor girl? The more she thought about it the angrier she got.

I ought to throw her out of here.

But Julie was her most popular girl. She didn't want to lose her. She didn't want to lose the money Julie brought in.

"Humph," Pauline grunted. *If Julie Cramer wants to be called Karen O'Day so what, it's no skin off my butt!*

With a combination of diminishing anger and a bit of affection, she shook her head and went to her office.

Julie ran up the steps and went to the bathroom. She gargled the sour taste of puke away and brushed her teeth. After wiping her mouth, she stood looking at her reflection in the mirror, running her fingers over her silky youthful looking skin. Pleased with the way she looked, she smiled vainly, and went to her room.

Once in the privacy of her bedroom, she locked the door, went to the closet and pulled a large cardboard box from the top shelf. She carried the box to her bed and dumped the contents on the quilt.

Hundreds of pictures and scribbled notes spilled out in front of her. She pushed the box aside and began shuffling through the pile, looking for the strip of self-portrait pictures she made in the photobooth at Beach Bend Park. She found the pose she was looking for, cut it from the strip, and placed it on the bed beside her. Stiff and tired from bending over she twisted the kinks from her back, stretched her legs, and then started looking for the old photo of Karen O'Day that she used as a model for the pose.

"Damn it, where is it?" she growled.

Frustrated, she pushed up off the bed and went to the window overlooking the parking lot. She lit a cigarette, smoked it half-way down, snubbed it out, and went back to the pile of prints lying on the bed and continued searching. Ten minutes later the photo flipped over in front of her.

"Ah! There it is," she whispered. "This is almost as exciting as the first time Professor Jones paid me for sex," she said with a quiet laugh.

Still chuckling, she taped both pictures on a sheet of pink letter paper. She studied the two prints for several minutes, and then went to her purse, retrieved the Polaroid she shot of Preston Desmond, and sat back down on the bed.

"*Mr.* Desmond, you looked straight at me when you walked out of the Hilltopper Restaurant totally unaware I was watching. You are an idiot."

She laughed as she taped the picture onto the paper. Perfect. She admired her handywork, smiled, and then taped the best photo she could find of Frederick Desmond. It was taken at the trial of Felix Curtis and it was a little fuzzy, but it would work. She chuckled smugly at her creation and began writing her letter.

When she finished writing she slipped the paper in an envelope and put the envelope in her purse. A giddy feeling of euphoria swept over her, almost like the feeling she felt the day she was baptized in the river on Granny's farm.

God, I miss those days, she thought with a sudden melancholy. The brief touch of guilt vanished as quickly as it arrived, replaced by the revenge taking shape in her mind.

Now, no one could deny what the pictures confirmed. Julie Cramer was truly the reincarnation of Karen O'Day. She was Karen O'Day.

There was knock on the door. "Karen?"

"Yes…"

"You have a date waiting for you."

Chapter 16

Thursday night Preston Desmond dreamed he was naked and tied to the bench, while a vaporous team of ghostly players ran over the Hilltoppers. The more he struggled to break free the deeper the chains coiled around his neck, tightening like a python, painfully strangling him.

Leading the crowd in the grisly nightmare like a beautiful demon from hell, danced Karen O'Day, twirling and prancing, laughing and singing, pointing at him and chanting, 'it's your fault Freddy Desmond…It's your fault Freddy Desmond!' Then, as if on cue, everyone in the stadium stood up and started shouting, 'it's your fault Freddy Desmond…It's your fault Freddy Desmond!'

Terrified, his heart pounding like a kick drum, he screamed for help, searching the mob for at least one sane person who go against the crowd and save him. Help came in the form of a squeaking door hinge.

He jerked awake grabbing at his throat with both hands. When he forced his eyes open, John Wayne McKinney was standing at the door, making the noise by swinging it back and forth with one hand, while the other held a textbook and a pink envelope. Letting go of the door, he tossed the envelope on top of Desmond's bed.

"Found this on the floor, Stud. It's got your name on it. Don't know who it's from."

Shaken by the dream, Preston rolled over, a queasy chill in his gut. He shook his head, took a deep breath, and sat up wiping the sleep from his eyes.

"Where are you going so early," he mumbled.

"To class, and it's not that early," JW said. "I thought you had an Accounting Lab this morning."

"Oh yeah," Preston said with weary insolent shrug. "I forgot."

JW's forehead narrowed, then immediately relaxed. He shook his head and looked down at his friend. "Prez, what the hell's the matter with you?"

When there was no reply, JW fought off the urge to pull Preston out of the bed and throw him against the wall. Instead of following his instincts he sighed, gritted his teeth, and slammed the door on his way out.

"What the hell's your problem?" Preston muttered after the big guy was gone.

He put his feet on the floor, leaned over with his elbows on his knees, and sat on the edge of the bed inexplicably frightened. His mind raced with disconnected thoughts. He was confused. His psychology class once skimmed over the subject of dream interpretation, but that was like reading a conceptual poem to a freshman lit class, then asking the group of eighteen-year-old kids to tell you what the poet was really saying. *Who the hell knows!*

"I'm acting like an idiot," he said half a loud, "a damn idiot!"

He threw the covers off to the side, and forced himself to his feet, ignoring the letter as it slipped to the floor. Lack of a restful sleep made him wobbly. He stumbled down the hall to the bathroom, took a cold shower, and returned twenty minutes later feeling a few degrees better.

He grabbed his pants and started putting them on when the pink envelope lying on the floor caught his eye. He picked it up. His name, beautifully written across the front of the envelope, gave him a chuckle.

Must be a note from Mona, he thought.

Then, lilacs and roses!

The hair on his arm bristled, the feeling of a second ago immediately replaced by a fearful dread. He ripped open the seal, put the envelope to his nose, and sniffed. His stomach dropped.

As he lifted the pink letter from the envelope an ominous darkness seemed to fill the room. Staring at him like two beautiful angels were two Karen O'Day's, a generation apart, both smiling at him. A nervous chuckle in his throat settled into a ball of dry cotton.

The bitter taste of rage crawled up his gullet, forcing the dry cotton onto his tongue. He swallowed it down and threw the letter on the floor, fighting the urge to hit the wall with his fist. Trembling with a mixture of anger and fear, he dropped kicked the desk, then yelled out in pain, flopping down on the bed rubbing his pulsating toe. When the ache eased, he picked up the letter and began reading:

My Dearest Freddy, or Preston if that's what you prefer.

I know what I'm about to tell you will be a shock, and I'm sure you'll deny it. You'll even say it's impossible. I know when I first realized the truth, I couldn't believe it either. But the truth is the truth, and the truth is my love, you are THE Freddy Desmond. Don't laugh, it is true.

My life has been an empty shell since the day I was born, and I didn't know why. Then one day I happened to see a program on television about this handsome young football player at my alma mater named Preston Desmond. I was so stunned, and oh, my, how thrilled it made my heart. Still, I didn't know why.

Of course, I knew about my Aunt Karen and Frederick, but I wasn't ready for the truth. You see, that was before I learned about reincarnation from Dr. Jones my history professor. Dr. Jones opened my eyes. He took one look at me and said I had to be Karen O'Day come back from the grave. Dr. Jones changed my life. He made me what I am today, but that's another story.

Freddy, I started keeping track of you after seeing the program on television. I followed you. You didn't know it, but I watched every move you made. I was attracted to you physically, but I passed that off as hormones.

I didn't understand how reincarnation applied to us until the night we met at the party. It wasn't until you walked into the room and looked at me that it hit like a bolt of lightning. Then, all the memories came flooding back. I knew at that moment that you, my love, are my Frederick Preston Desmond.

If you don't believe me look at the pictures. You can't deny them. No one can deny it. Two people cannot be that identical unless they are twins. Well, my darling no set of twins are born thirty-five years apart.

I knew long before the party that I am Karen O'Day, and that we would meet again. That night I realized I'd finally found you.

You are mine Freddy. I will not share you with anyone, especially that bitch Mona Cooper. You'd better do something about her, Freddy! You better do something quick! We both know you've done it before! You belong to me. We belong together.

Do not refuse to believe it this time. You refused to believe it in 1920. You refused to believe it when you got me pregnant. You refused to believe it, and you killed me! You killed the only woman who ever really loved you. But Freddy I forgive you, because I still love you, because---YOU BELONG TO ME!

Have a good day,

Karen, hugs and kisses XOXOXOXOXOXOXOOXOX

PS: Oh yes, I almost forgot. Silly me...but of course you remember how forgetful I am. I will be spending Saturday night at the bridge. If you care, be there---BE THERE!

"My God, the woman's insane!" Preston grumbled smacking his forehead several times with the palm of his hand. "What the hell have I gotten into?"

He put the letter back in the envelope and jammed it in his pocket just as a loud rap on the door sent a cold stab shooting through his chest. He stood momentarily frozen when a second louder pounding shook the mirror on the wall.

"Preston are you in there?" Mona Cooper shouted. "Preston…!"

"Mona?"

"Yes! Open the door!"

The tension building in him released like an uncoiled spring. He rushed across the room, swung the door open, and yanked Mona inside. She jerked out of his grip rubbing the back of her neck with both hands.

"What the hell is…?" The pale look etched across his face instantly squashed her anger. "My God, Preston, what's wrong with you? You look terrible."

Without answering, he moved to the doorway, eased his head around the doorframe, and peaked down the dimly lit hall. Taking a second look to be sure no one was there he looked both ways then shut and locked the door.

"Preston, you're scaring me." Mona said softly. "I want to know right now, tell me… what's happening."

He pulled the crumbled envelope from his pocket, handed her the letter, and sat down on the edge of the bed. Mona read it, grunted at the photographs, and then tossed the letter on the desk.

"You don't believe any of this garbage, do you?"

"I don't know."

Mona groaned. "There's no such thing as reincarnation, Preston."

"A lot of people believe in it."

"That doesn't make it true."

"Then how do you explain Bridey Murphy?" Preston said.

"Who's Bridey Murphy? I've never heard of her," Mona said.

"Don't you read anything besides *Cosmopolitan?*"

"This is not about me," Mona snapped. "Who's Bridey Murphy?"

"She was a young girl who lived in Ireland in the 1700's," he said, "A woman who lived somewhere in Colorado about 10 or 15 years ago claimed to be the reincarnation of her, of Bridey Murphy."

"So now, because someone wrote an article in a magazine about a goof ball in Colorado, you believe it."

"Mona, when the woman was hypnotized, she remembered things. She remembered stuff she had no way of knowing. The doctors were stumped, and a few of them even said they believed her. If the doctors believed her, how can you say Karen O'Day isn't who she says she is?"

Mona gave a frustrated sigh. "I can say it's not true, because…it's not true!" She sat down beside him and took his hand in hers. "Preston, how long have we known each other?"

Preston shrugged. "Four years?"

"Yes, four years. And in all that time you've been the one person who's always taken control of situations. If something came up, you were the one who was strong, the one so sure of himself. Sometimes that got annoying as could be, but it was also rather comforting."

She paused and squeezed his hand. "My love, all your life everything has always come too easy for you. Nothing ever bothers you. At times, your confidence has been to the point of arrogance." There was a rough edge taking hold in her voice.

Preston pulled his hand away from hers. "Where are you going with this?"

She rose to her feet, standing so close their legs touched, her arms across her chest, her eyes boring into his. "Where do you think, I'm going?" she snapped. "You act like a scared little boy and I don't like it. Ever since you met that bitch you've been acting like a puppy dog with his tail tucked between his legs. Where is the strong courageous man I fell in love with? Where's your backbone!"

She moved quickly to the door and took hold of the doorknob, squeezing so tightly her knuckles turned white.

"Now get up and stand on your own two feet. We've got a bigger problem to deal with. That bitch threatened to kill me, and I'm not going to put up with it. Give me the letter, we're going to the police."

Chapter 17

Still seething, thanks to Karen O'Day's insane communiqué, Mona Cooper marched into the Bowling Green Police Department geared for battle. Preston Desmond lagged a few steps behind. Still feeling uneasy, he stopped just inside the door and leaned against the wall.

The dark beige color scheme of the police department's front office created an oppressive atmosphere. The dull, battleship grey, metal desk standing in front of the far wall didn't help lighten the feel. Two wire trays, one marked *in* the other labeled *out*, set on the right-hand side of the desk. A black telephone was on the left.

A skinny female receptionist wearing a tan colored sheriff's auxiliary uniform sat behind the desk. She was busy working her jaws on a stick of chewing gum with the telephone receiver plastered to her ear. The plastic tag on her blouse said her name was Lorraine.

Mona stood with her arms folded across her chest, tapping her foot while holding her breath against the pungent smell coming from Lorraine's sweat stained uniform. When Lorraine finally hung up the phone, she looked up at Mona with the simile of a smile and adjusted her plastic ink-smudged white frame glasses.

"Yes?" she said in nasally monotone.

"I need to see a policeman," Mona said.

"What for?" nasal replied.

"I want to see an officer!" Mona said more vocally.

"And why, do you need to see a policeman?" Lorraine repeated, the hint of a spiteful sneer tipping the corner of her thin lips.

"Just get me a damn cop!" Mona shouted.

Lorraine's face turned a bright crimson red. She was about to shout back, when a tall, wiry looking man, with steel-gray hair on his head, and sergeant's stripes on his sleeve, hurried into the room.

"What's going on out here, Lorraine?" he said, the wide nostrils on his long nose flaring out like broad sails on a racing schooner. "What's all the noise about?"

"This lady," Lorraine said jabbing a thumb toward Mona. "She wants to see a policeman. When I asked her what the problem was, she yelled at me."

"I did *not* yell at you!" Mona objected.

"You did so, I was just trying to do my job."

"I did not!"

"I heard you all the way in the back of the office, Miss…"

"Cooper, Mona Cooper."

"Okay, Miss Cooper. You did get a bit loud. Now, why don't you tell me the problem. Why do you need to see a police officer?"

"Someone threatened to kill me," Mona said glancing at his name tag. "That is the problem, *Sergeant* Johnson!"

"Who threatened to kill you, Miss Cooper?" Johnson said, scratching his head while his eyes wandered fitfully around the room. It was clear he didn't give a flip about Mona's problem until he noticed Western Kentucky's football hero standing by the door.

"Well, I'll be damn, Preston Desmond! What are you doing out so late? Don't you have a ballgame tomorrow?"

Preston shook his head and stepped away from the wall. "We don't have a game this week, Sergeant," he said.

"Well, you get in bed early anyhow. We need you in tiptop condition out on that field." He grinned and scratched his chin whiskers. "You know, I was at the game last week, and I swear, boy, I've never seen anybody run as fast as you do." He paused and laughed. "That is unless they're running away from us."

Preston forced a halfhearted chuckle. "That's what I do, Sergeant. I run away from the big boys."

Johnson sniffed through his left nostril and puckered up his face like Barney Fife. "Yeah, I know what you mean. I played linebacker in high school. It's tough going up against them big boys. Some of those guys get huge."

"Sergeant Johnson," Mona said sharply, the veins in her neck pulsating in rhythm with the ball of her foot beating on the floor. "If you don't mind, I'd like to file a complaint!"

The Sergeant's schooner sails flared again, his lips pressing into a wide slit imitating a grin. "I'll get an officer right with you, Miss Cooper." He jabbed the intercom button with his middle finger, and growled, "Watkins, come to the front desk?"

He glanced icily at Mona, and then turned back to Preston, the smile jumping back into place. "Son, you think you could give me a couple of autographs for my boys. They think you're the greatest thing to run on a football field since Paul Hornung. Someday, when you're in the Hall of Fame with him in Canton your autographs will be valuable."

"I don't know about that," Preston said taking the proffered pad and pen from Johnson. He scribbled his name on two sheets and handed the pad back to the sergeant. "But I hope you're right."

"You need me, Sarge?" Detective James Watkins asked as he came around the corner into the room. He was a tall lean man with a swarthy complexion, square jaw, serious eyes. His sculptured features emphasized a classic Roman nose. He walked up smiling pleasantly at Mona and Preston.

"Yes, we do, Jim," Johnson said. "How about taking Miss Cooper back to your desk and help her fill out some paperwork. She wants to file a complaint. She thinks somebody threatened to kill her."

At the *she thinks* remark Mona sucked in a deep infuriated breath. She puffed up like a cobra spreading its hood, the muscles rippling across her cheeks. Before she could say something that might blow up into an ugly scene Preston grabbed her arm and squeezed. She bit her tongue and backed away.

Feeling the animosity building, Preston stepped between the two and reached out his hand.

"Sergeant Johnson, Mona and I appreciate your help," he said. "And as a thank you, I'll see if I can get you a couple of tickets for our next game."

Although Johnson smiled affably, his yellowish-green reptilian eyes grabbed Preston contemptuously. "Why don't you try to get six," he said taking the offered hand and squeezing like it was a knuckle breaking contest. "Me and the boys here at the station always do what we can for the Big Red."

You're an asshole, Preston thought. He put on a friendly grin and said, "I'll see what I can do."

"That's good," Johnson said. "I look forward to the game."

While Sergeant Johnson was trying to wheedle more free football tickets out of Desmond, Detective Watkins touched Mona's arm and motioned her to follow him. Mona grabbed Preston's hand and pulled him away from Johnson. Together they followed the detective down a brightly lit hallway, turned right at the second door, and walked into an office area about the size of a two-car garage.

Two rows of four desks each packed the room with just enough space to walk between. Watkins indicated Mona sit in the chair next to his desk, and then he pulled a stool over for Preston. When all three were seated Mona took the crumpled envelope from her purse.

"This is a letter Preston received this morning," she said placing it on the desk in front of Watkins. "It's from a woman who claims her name is Karen

O'Day. Somebody, I guess it was her, slid the thing under his door at Sandstone Manor."

Watkins studied the beautiful calligraphy on the envelope for a long moment, lifting his eyebrows in appreciation, before opening the flap and removing the crinkled piece of paper.

"As you can see," Mona said. "The woman is obviously a nut case. She thinks she's reincarnated from a girl who was murdered at a covered bridge somewhere in Warren County forty-five years ago. The dead girl's name was Karen O'Day. Now, if that isn't crazy, I don't know what is."

Watkins nodded. "I know the case. We studied it at the police academy. It's known as the covered bridge murder. Back in the 1920's it was a big case that troubled the entire state."

"Well, that's not the half of it," Mona said. "She is so delusional she thinks Preston Desmond was the killer." She paused and pointed to the middle of the page. "Right here she tells him if he could do it once, I think you know what that means, if he can do it once, he can do it again. She is demanding he kill me. She is *completely* out of her mind! Read it, and then tell me she's not crazy!" She sat up straight in the chair, staring holes in Watkins. "I want her arrested!"

Detective Watkins read the letter, and when he finished, he placed the sheet on the desk, and leaned back in his chair nodding his head. He sat quietly for a full minute, watching the couple's movements as if they were suspects in a bank heist. Preston sat calmly, but Mona squirmed and fidgeted around on the chair like it was shooting electric shocks in her butt.

Finally, Watkins formed a temple with his fingers, the beginning traces of a somber smile forming on his face. He looked at Mona, and then settled on Preston.

"Preston," he said. "Have you ever been to Pauline's?"

"Where?"

"Pauline's."

"The *whorehouse?*"

"Yes."

"Hell no!" Preston said surprised at the question.

"What's that got to do with any of this?" Mona snapped, the blood rushing to her face.

"Relax," he said, holding up one hand palm out. "I don't care if you've been to the whorehouse, or not. But I have a reason for asking." He turned the letter face up and tapped his index finger on the newest picture. "This woman is a thirty-year-old prostitute at Pauline's brothel." He paused, watching Preston's eyes increase in diameter. "Her real name is Julie Cramer."

"No way," Preston sputtered.

"That doesn't surprise me one bit," Mona said.

"You've got to be kidding," Preston said.

"No, I'm deadly serious," Watkins said. "Julie Cramer has been selling her wares at Pauline's for about eight months or so. That's why I wanted to know if you'd ever been there. I think it could be where she first saw you." Preston didn't respond and Watkins turned to Mona. "Miss Cooper, some male students visit with Pauline from time to time just to talk, and to dance with the pretty girls. The boys can't afford to do anything else, and Pauline likes to have them come in."

"*Right*," Mona scoffed "I'm sure they just go to talk."

"Preston, did you ever go there…just to talk and dance?"

"I told you, I've never been there…"

Watkins nodded skeptically. "Okay."

"Detective, that woman said she first saw Preston on a television program."

"Yeah, well…maybe she did," Watkins said.

Preston rested back in the chair, staring at Watkins. "She seemed so sweet, so friggin' normal."

"Being a prostitute doesn't make her any less a person," Watkins said.

"I know that. What I meant to say was she looks crazy now, but then…when I first met her…she…oh, I don't know, I just have a hard time believing it."

Watkins rose from his desk, went to a row of file cabinets at the rear of the room. He shuffled through the files and came back a few moments later carrying a manila folder. He dropped the folder on the desk, sat down, and flipped the cover open.

"Okay, now," he said lifting a sheet from the file folder. "Julie Cramer has been arrested for prostitution in Louisville, Nashville, New Orleans and Indianapolis. We arrested her in Bowling Green twice for drunken driving. That's how we learned she worked at Pauline's. Pauline came in and paid Julie's fines.

"Her arrest record for prostitution goes back almost eight years. It started when she was a student up on the hill."

"Was she working at Pauline's when she was in school?" Preston asked.

"No. We don't have any records or reports of a coed ever working at the brothel. Julie got into the business in 1957, when a history professor on the hill named Robert Jones got the bright idea that he could put Pauline out of business. He started running a stable of coeds."

"Robert Jones? Was that the same man who co-wrote the history of Bowling Green book with Maude Semonian?" Mona asked.

"The one and the same," Watkins grunted. "Professor Jones was a strange bird. People claim he was a genius, and from what I've heard he was respected by scholars across the country. He wrote several history books and dime store novels, mostly romance and light porn. But he was also a pimp who exploited young women.

"I think he had seven coeds working for him, and, for a brief time he had quite a business going. Julie was his first girl." He paused and displayed a mystified smile. "It still amazes me how he was able to recruit Julie. She was brought up in a good home, popular in high school, and was even voted most beautiful in her senior class. Her family wasn't wealthy by any means, but they were comfortable." He shrugged. "I don't know, I guess she just likes to…huh…likes what she does."

"And the administration never knew, or found out, he was running escorts?" Preston asked.

"No, not until after he was killed." Watkins said. "His walk on the wild side only lasted about a year. He was killed while attending a history seminar in St. Louis. The shooter has never been caught." He paused again and looked curiously at Preston. "I'm surprised you've never heard of Professor Jones' Topper Girls. It wasn't that long ago, about seven years."

"No, this is the first I've heard about that," Preston said shaking his head. "It's still hard for me to believe that she's a hooker, period. I mean she's so young looking and so beautiful."

"She's not that beautiful," Mona scoffed. "She's a lunatic who wants me dead!"

Watkins tapped Karen's picture with his finger. "The way this letter reads I would agree Julie is a shade out of the ordinary, Miss Cooper. But she didn't actually threaten to kill you."

"It sounds like a threat to me," Mona said.

"I understand how you feel. I really do. But nowhere in the letter does it say she is going to kill you. In fact, the only place she even mentions killing is when she refers to the covered bridge murder in 1920. In other words, nothing she says gives us a reason to arrest her."

He put the letter back in the envelope, and instead of handing it to Preston casually slipped it in the manila folder. He gave Mona his business card and stood up extending his hand.

"If you do hear anything more from her, or you have any more problems call me."

"We'll do that. Thank you, detective," Preston said. They shook hands, and as they walked by Lorraine's desk Preston smiled at her and mouthed "Have a good night."

Lorraine's admiring eyes never left Preston as he walked out the door.

Out on the sidewalk Mona gave the detective's card to Preston. "That was a complete waste of time," she said. "Take me home."

Chapter 18

Parked on the street less than a block away from the police station, Julie Cramer slouched behind the wheel of the blue Ford and chuckled sarcastically at how predictable people could be. It amazed her how easy it was to follow people. They were so oblivious to their surroundings it was funny. They were totally unaware of everything going on around them. They were like…like lambs to the slaughter.

"Yeah, that's what you are, bitch. You're like a lamb to the slaughter. That's where you're going Mona," she mumbled angrily. "You're going to the slaughter. But you ain't no lamb, darlin'. You're a fucking pig, and Preston the 'Super Star' Desmond doesn't know it yet, but he's gonna do the slaughtering."

"God, I'm bored. I couldn't be a cop…stakeouts would bore me to the point of suicide. I wish I smoked," she said mumbling in the air. "At least smoking a cigarette would give me something to do. Sitting in the dark, alone, waiting to see a couple of idiots is boring as hell." She reached in her purse, pulled out a pack of Spearmint gum and popped a stick in her mouth.

"What the hell could they be doing in there," she growled. "Shit! Now I'm talking to myself. Who cares? What's taking them so long? Damn! Stupid bitch. What does Preston Desmond see in a plain Jane nobody like that Mona Bologna? Hey, that's a good one," she said louder than she meant. Still giggling, she covered her mouth and mumbled, "I like that…Mona Bologna."

The doors to the police station opened and Mona Cooper walked out followed closely behind by Preston Desmond.

"Oh, Preston. You are such a pussy," she muttered. "God! What a wimp! Why don't you just let her put a ring in your nose and lead you around like a pet bull? No, that's not right, a bull's strong and hard to control. You're easy, you follow her around like ah…ah…a whipped puppy, that's it, a puppy. Puppy dog Preston! Ah! What a joke. It won't be long now Preston, until you pay for what you did to me."

She glanced up at her reflection in the rearview mirror and recoiled, horrified at the image glaring back.

"Oh God!" she screamed.

Deep tight stretch lines etched her eyes. Water poured off her head and down her face, her hair plastered on her head.

Frantically, she squished her eyes tight, grabbing her hair with both hands. Then, just as suddenly, her eyes snapped open and hesitantly, she peered in the mirror. Her hair was dry, no water, only stiff hair spray. She touched gently at her eyes. The skin was smooth, no wrinkles. She let out a deep relieved sigh as her beautiful reflection stared back.

Tears ran down her cheeks as she lowered her head and cried. "Oh, Freddy. Why did you do this to me?" She sat crying for several minutes.

When she looked up Preston Desmond and Mona Cooper were nowhere in sight. Standing in front of the police station was a man she recognized as a detective she had seen before. He stood smoking a cigarette and appeared to be looking toward the college. He dropped the butt on the ground, crushed it under his shoe, and then went back inside.

She dried her eyes and fired up the engine. She looked both ways, then turned the car around, and made a right on Center Street toward the college.

Chapter 19

Detective Watkins leaned back in his chair and watched Desmond and Cooper walk out the door. After they were gone, he walked outside and lit a cigarette. He watched the Corvette move up College Street. When it made a right turn and out of sight, he dropped the half-finished butt on the sidewalk, crushed it out with the toe of his shoe, and walked back to his desk.

He settled back on his chair and removed the letter from the envelope, unfolded it, and sat staring at the pictures. He didn't believe in any of the paranormal bull crap that was currently in vogue, but how could you explain the two women in the pictures. They looked identical. *Who knows* he thought, *maybe there is something to it?* "Nah!"

He put the letter back in the envelope, tossed it to the side of the desk, and lit a cigarette; he took a deep drag, and then blew the smoke toward the overhead light. The whole situation bugged him. He shook his head. A detective develops a sixth sense, an intuition, a feeling, whatever the hell you want to call it when something isn't right, and right now his gut was telling him this ain't right.

He leaned forward, thumbed through the Rolodex stopping at the file card he kept on Pauline Tabor. He pulled the card out of the holder, and sat for a full minute, cigarette in one hand, the other tapping the edge of the card on the desk. After several minutes arguing with himself about whether to call her or not, he reached for the phone.

Pauline answered in two rings.

"Hello?"

"Ms. Tabor?"

"Yes…"

"Ma'am, I'm Detective James Watkins with the Bowling Green Police."

A brief silence before she said, "Yes…what can I do for you, detective?"

"Ma'am, does Julie Cramer still work for you?"

Another hesitation. "What is this all about Detective? Has Julie broken the law?"

The irony of the remark made him chuckle. He wiped the smile off his face with his hand, and said, "Pauline, we've had a complaint that Julie Cramer threatened to kill a young female student at Western. Now we know you have a professional relationship with Julie Cramer. Do you think she's capable of killing someone?"

"Detective, I think anyone is capable of killing another person if given the right motivation. But as far as knowing much about Julie, I don't. she's only been with me for a few months. She stays to herself and doesn't socialize with the other girls." She paused and chuckled acidly. "I wouldn't be surprised to learn she didn't even know some of the other girl's names. She's a loner."

"So, you don't know anything about her background?"

"I know she graduated from up on the hill, and that she'd been arrested a couple of times for prostitution. Other than that, no, I don't know anything. Like I said, she came here about, what…maybe eight months ago. I took one look at her, and you know she is extraordinarily beautiful, and I said to myself, 'honey if you pass the medical, you've got a job.' She passed with a clean bill of health. That's all I know about her."

"Umm," Watkins said. "I think I need to talk to her. I'm going to drop by your place---"

"You'll be wasting your time, detective. She's not here. I haven't seen her."

"You have any idea where she could be?"

"None at all."

After he hung up the phone Watkins went to the front desk and put out a BOLO, (be on the lookout) for Julie Cramer. What she is wearing and driving unknown.

Chapter 20

After taking Mona Cooper to breakfast at Denny's Restaurant on the by-pass, Preston pulled up in front of her dorm and turned off the engine. He reached over and gently squeezed her hand.

"I'll pick you up about five-thirty," he said. "We'll have a romantic dinner in Nashville and maybe go to a couple of clubs. How does that sound?"

"Absolutely wonderful," Mona whispered with a sexy smile. "We need to get away. I can't wait." She leaned over, kissed him twice, then opened the door and hurried out.

As soon as she was safely in the dorm, Preston gritted his teeth angrily, and squealed the Goodyear tires pulling out of the parking lot and sped down College Street. It was time to settle the Julie Cramer problem once and for all.

He made a quick left onto Main Street, bounced roughly over the railroad tracks, and made a tight right on Clay Street. The milk can was not in the middle of the driveway. He pulled his Corvette behind the brick building and came to a stop next to a shiny new black Lincoln Continental. He sat quietly staring at the expensive car for several minutes wondering who the VIP visiting the brothel might be.

"Who cares," he mumbled shrugging indifferently.

John Wayne had offered to come with him, he claimed for moral support, but Preston knew that was a load of crap. He just wanted an excuse to visit the girls. "I should have brought you, John," he grunted.

He opened the car door, and a swarm of butterflies suddenly attacked his stomach. Nervous jitters. Worse than before a football game. Why? He was just going into a whore house. So, what? He'd never been in a whore house before. Maybe that's was it. But why should that make him nervous. Maybe the whores intimidated him. Why, women loved him. Maybe it was because he'd heard Pauline was a tough old lady who wouldn't tolerate trouble. Well, trouble was the last thing he wanted.

Chuckling to himself, he used a self-manipulating trick his mother taught him and reached up beside his head, acted like he was grabbing the fear and anxiety in his fist, and then mentally threw it away. Amazingly, it always seemed to work. He took a deep breath, pushed up out of the Corvette and slammed the car door.

Surprisingly, the temperature had dropped several degrees since the sun came up, and the cold air hitting his face was like stepping into a meat locker. He tightened the jacket around his neck and hurried to the rear door of the bordello. The butterflies danced to a faster tune in his gut as he opened the door and stepped into the small foyer.

Only two of Pauline's girls were in sight. One, a slender young platinum blonde wearing a white see through blouse, a black bra, and white jeans was staring intently into a jukebox that stood next to the wall on the left. She dropped in a coin and pushed the selection buttons. The 45-rpm record dropped into place, and Santo and Johnny's *Sleep Walk* filled the room with a warm sexy mood. Swaying seductively with the music, she danced across the room, her bare pedicured feet sliding, one two three, with the melody. At the sofa she did a classical pirouette and settled daintily on the couch.

Next to her reclined a renaissance plump woman who appeared to be in her late 20's. She was wearing a pale pink t-shirt, that clashed with her bright red hair, and white panties with matching garter belt attached to fishnet stockings. She looked bored masticating a wad of chewing gum aggressively, while filing her nails with the same force. The cold air, rushing through the door, raised goose bumps on her forearms, turning the skin pinkish blue.

Both women looked up when Preston walked in and offered a well-practiced friendly welcome.

"Well, hello good-looking," the blonde, with the platinum locks, said rising from the sofa. "My name is Jade. What can I do for you?" Her soft voice killed the butterflies torturing Preston's guts.

Turning on the Desmond charm he puffed out his chest and started to make a suggestive reply but quickly caught himself.

Remember why you're here, Prez. "I'd like to see Julie Cramer," he said.

"Another one for Julie," the redhead muttered under her breath, obviously irritated.

"Julie's not here," said a voice behind him.

Preston turned to see Pauline standing by the door. He hadn't heard the door, or felt the cold air blowing in.

Pauline finger-combed her grey hair that was mussed by the wind and slipped off her dark blue overcoat. She was wearing a faded green cotton dress, the kind he'd seen his granny wearing when she worked in her garden. It covered her short round body loosely. She hung the coat on the rack standing in the corner next to the door and approached him. She reminded him of his grandma.

"Jade and Wendy are available," Pauline said with a warm down-home smile. "They're both sweet girls, and just as good as Julie."

Preston chuckled. "I'm sure they are, Miss Pauline. But I really need to speak to Julie Cramer, it's important."

"Honey, either one of these girls can make you forget about Julie in five minutes."

"I really need to talk to Julie Cramer," Preston said more forcefully than he intended. The sweet as sugar grandmother's smile vanished from Pauline's face, morphing into a somber, pick a girl or get the hell out, madam.

"Well, good luck with that, dear," she growled. "When I said Julie is not here, what I meant to say is, she is no longer one of my girls. Julie packed her bags and slipped away in the middle of the night, didn't so much as say kiss my ass."

"And you don't have any idea where she went?"

Pauline's eyes clouded over resembling dark cold rocks. She formed a 'you idiot' look on her face, and said, "What do you think, darlin'? How would I know where she's going, if I had no idea that she was leaving?" She began moving toward the hallway, but suddenly stopped and turned back slowly, fixing him with an incredulous stare. She held the pose for several seconds, then grunted an unintelligible remark and proceeded down the hall.

Preston watched her walk away. Feeling like a fool he went to the door and grabbed the doorknob.

"Wait a minute, darling," Jade called, her fingertip toying with her bottom lip. "Don't leave yet. We can still have a party."

Preston shook his head timidly. "Not today, honey. Not today." He pulled his collar tight and stepped out into the cold.

Chapter 21

The sun was low in the west when Preston parked the vette in the Sandstone Manor parking lot and walked the few hundred yards up the hill to the Hilltopper. Since there was no game this week several of the football team had congregated in the restaurant. John Wayne McKinney waved Preston to the table near the far back wall. He was sitting with teammates Sam Pushin and Ed Stanton.

Sam played right guard. He was only five-ten, but had shoulders like anvils, and at 230 pounds he was built like a bull, and strong as an ox.

Ed Stanton was a walk-on center who followed Sam around like a shadow. He also thought everything he said was either hilarious or provocative.

Preston edged through the crowd and joined them. He grabbed a chair from another table, slid it between JW and Sam, and slumped down.

"Well, how did it go this morning, Prez," JW asked. "Did you get that nut case straightened out?"

"No," Preston said, shaking his head. He leaned forward, resting his elbows on the table. "She's gone, doesn't work there anymore. The old lady said she snuck out in the middle of the night. She has no idea where she went."

"Who's the nut case, Mona Cooper?" Ed Stanton chuckled as he punched Sam Pushin playfully on the shoulder.

"Ouch!" Sam flinched, and punched Ed back, this time much harder. The café owner standing behind the cash register saw the exchange and glared at both, scowling his disapproval.

"No, not Mona," John Wayne said. "Preston's got a crazy fan. She's drop-dead gorgeous, but a couple-a eggs short of a dozen."

"Hey, I don't mind crazy," Ed said with an imitation of a grin. "I like weird broads. Give her my phone number. After one night with me she'll forget all about Mr. Hilltopper."

The remark had the sour smell of jealousy like limburger cheese on a raw onion. No one laughed.

"I doubt that Ed," Preston grunted. "She's one of Pauline's girls. I think she's had more than enough schlongs to compare ours with."

Stanton's chin dropped for a split second before 'one of Pauline's girls' suddenly dawned on him. His head shot up and he laughed loudly turning heads at surrounding tables.

"Wait a minute!" he yelled, loud enough to keep the on-looker's attention "You mean one of Pauline's whores has the hots for Preston? Oh, man! Now that's funny! One of Pauline's whores is in love with the campus stud! That is friggin' great!"

"Quit being such a smart-ass, Ed," JW said. "She may be a whore, but she's still a woman, a human being!"

"Oh, screw her," Stanton said. "It's still funny."

Stanton's remarks were rapidly reaching the breaking point.

"It's not a damn bit funny, Ed," Preston said, lowering his voice a couple of decibels. He squared his shoulders, and looked around the table, meeting each man's eyes with a hard stare. "Julie Cramer is really off the deep end. So, this morning I went over to Pauline's to try and straighten her out once and for all. She wasn't there, she's gone; no longer works there."

"Yeah, I'll bet you were going to straighten her out," Ed Stanton said with a coarse chuckle.

"Knock it off, Ed. That crap's getting old," John Wayne growled.

"I'm serious, guys. I think she's a psychopath," Preston said.

"Whoa…" Sam Pushin muttered.

"Has she done something else?" JW asked.

"Yeah, John," Preston said turning his eyes to his roommate. "She wants me to kill Mona Cooper."

A hushed silence thick as wet fog surrounded the table. It was broken when Sam Pushin said quietly, "You're not kidding, are you?"

"No Sam, I'm serious as a heart attack."

"Man, that's heavy," Ed Stanton said, suddenly out of witty remarks.

"When did this happen?" John Wayne asked.

"It was in the letter you found under the door yesterday morning. Mona and I took it to the police last night. But that was a waste of gas. They said the writer didn't threaten anyone.

"That's also when we found out that Karen, or whatever her real name is, is really just a psychotic whore. Detective Watkins said she'd been arrested in several cities." Preston paused, looked at his watch, and then with a tired, dejected sigh, leaned back in the chair. "It's almost five o'clock. I told Mona I'd take her to Nashville tonight. Hopefully we can forget about this crap for a while."

"When were you supposed to pick her up?" Ed asked.

"5:30," Preston said. "Why?"

"Just curious," Ed said with a slight shrug. "I saw her getting into a light blue Ford when I was on my way over here."

Preston glanced restlessly at his watch again. "Damn, it's a quarter after five now, where would she be going at this hour?" The wheels in his brain started spinning like a mix master. "Who drives a blue Ford, JW? Do you know?"

John Wayne shook his head. "I don't have any idea."

"Who could that be...?" Preston muttered mostly to himself.

"I don't know who she was," Ed said, "but the woman driving the car was a smokin' hot brunette."

Sam Pushin scrunched his eyes tight, tapping his forehead with his fingertips. A moment later his eyes sprang wide open. "You know," he said "I've seen a pale blue Ford cruising around Sandstone Manor several times the past few weeks. In fact, I saw it again last night. I couldn't see the driver, but I do remember that big blue Ford."

Ed Stanton snapped his fingers. "Wait a minute! That girl! You know, the one you left the party with the other night. The brunette that looks like Natalie Wood."

"Yeah, what about her?" Preston was getting more uneasy by the minute. "What does she have to do with it?"

"She drives a blue Ford," Ed said.

The hair on Preston's neck bristled like a parade of nerve mites were crawling up his spine.

"How do you know that, Ed?" he asked a slight edge in his voice.

"I saw her yesterday at Jerry's drive-in restaurant, the one out on the by-pass. She was in a pale blue Ford Fairlane, one of those big mothers. I think it's a 1960," he smiled remembering what he'd hoped would happen. "She was alone, so you know, I figured I'd walk over and introduce myself. Tell her I was your good friend. Thought I'd slide in on your coattail." He lifted one eyebrow and shrugged. "But she left before I had a chance."

The realization of what was happening hit Preston in the gut like a punch from Muhammad Ali.

"Oh my God!" he said grabbing the edge of the table. He shot straight up to his feet, shoving the table forward into Ed Stanton's stomach. Stanton gasped an *umph*, and kicked his feet forward, shoving Preston's chair backward, hitting John Wayne on the shoulder.

"*Oww*, damn it!" John Wayne shouted rubbing his shoulder.

"John," Preston shouted, "I need you to come with me. Julie Cramer has Mona. We've got to get to that covered bridge, fast!"

"Why the covered bridge?"

"That's where Julie Cramer is taking Mona."

"Why would she take Mona there?" JW asked, still massaging his shoulder.

"Because, Karen O'Day was murdered on that bridge forty-five years ago today. Julie Cramer thinks she's that murdered girl."

"Well that's nuts!"

"Nuts ain't the word for it. Cramer really believes she's been reincarnated," Preston said. "That's why I'm sure the bridge is where she's taking Mona. She plans to kill her."

"Oh, fuck…" John Wayne groaned. Grabbing his coat and jumping to his feet he tossed two dollars on the table and pushed his chair out of the way. He side stepped another chair and rushed past three tables of students startled by the commotion.

"Pushin, come here!" Preston said as he pulled out his wallet and retrieved Detective Watkins' business card. He grabbed Sam Pushin by the arm and thrust the card in his hand.

"Sam, I need you to call Detective James Watkins and tell him Julie Cramer's got Mona Cooper. Tell him we think she's going to that old covered bridge out of Old Franklin Road, the one where Karen O'Day was murdered back in 1920. He'll know what you're talking about."

"I'm on it, Prez!" Sam yelled. He pushed away from the table and hurried to the pay phone hanging on the wall next to the cash register.

"Come on, John," Preston yelled as he hurried out the door.

A few minutes later he was at the bottom of Hilltop Drive, bent over, panting for breath. Seconds later John Wayne stumbled to a stop, his face crimson with red blotches, gasping for air.

"You okay, John?"

"Yeah…I'm…fine."

"Are you sure? You look like you're about to have a stroke."

JW tried to chuckle, but only gasped. "I play…on…the line. We only run about 6 seconds at a time." They stood on the corner for several seconds, waiting for his face to stop looking like it was about to explode. After a couple of minutes, he grinned, straightened his back and took two deep breaths. "Okay, brother," he said. "Let's go get Mona."

They took off at a run, slowing down to dodge two cars that were racing up College Heights Boulevard. They turned on the afterburners until they reached

Sandstone Manor's parking lot. Preston unlocked the Corvette, got in, and in one motion reached over and unlocked the passenger door. He grabbed the stenographer's notebook from the glove box and handed it to JW.

"I wrote the directions to the bridge in here. Make sure I don't miss a turn."

He turned the ignition key and the 327 cubic inch engine sprung to life like a sleeping dragon. He grabbed the gear shift, stomped the accelerator, and peeled out onto College Heights Boulevard. He stomped on the gas and fishtailed left onto State Street. The tires squealed again turning right on 14th Avenue East.

A road crew had traffic blocked at Greenwood, so he made a quick right onto Kenton Street. A two-car fender bender slowed him down at 15th. He hissed an irritated sigh, made a left turn, and then breathed a relieved sigh when the streets cleared.

Once they were onto the by-pass John Wayne looked at the road map. "Scottsville Road is the next turn," he said.

Preston nodded. "Yeah, I know."

They drove north on the highway for several minutes.

"There it is," John said pointing ahead. "State Road 231, Scottsville Road. Turn right."

Outside the city limits a thick blanket of fog gave everything an eerie look, the kind you see in old Sherlock Holmes movies. The aureole around the moon casted a ghostly haze creating a mountain of black vaporous clouds, turning the landscape into a scene out of the Hound of the Baskervilles. All that was needed was an enormous snarling dog.

John Wayne McKinney leaned against the dashboard trying to identify the figures that eerily seemed to be beckoning from the foggy countryside. Everything looked like marooned time travelers. The strain was making his eyes play tricks on him. He closed his tired eyes, rubbed them with both hands, then continued the search for the cemetery.

They drove quietly for several miles when Preston suddenly broke the silence and slowed the Vette to a rapid walk.

"John..." he said.

"Yeah?"

"I think that's it up ahead?"

"I don't see anything."

"About fifty yards on the right, just this side of that stand of trees." Preston said as pulled the car to the side of the road and came to a stop. He motioned toward four stones with rounded tops reflecting moonlight. "Right there," he said pointing toward a patch of weeds. "That's the cemetery! This is where we turn!"

He stomped the accelerator and made an abrupt left turn across S.R. 231, and bounced over the shoulder onto what appeared to be the crumbling asphalt of a long-forgotten road. Ten yards off the main highway he stopped the car. He reached under the seat, pulled out a flashlight, and handed it to JW.

"Stay here," Preston said. "When the cops come, flag them in. I'm going to the bridge. I only pray I'm not too late."

"I don't think that's a good idea, Brother. You shouldn't go alone. That O'Day broad is crazy. Two of us stand a better chance of saving Mona, especially if O'Day has a gun."

"I know you're right, JW," Preston said gripping the steering wheel tightly. "But look at this place. There's not a sign of a road anywhere. Maude said most people now days don't even remember a covered bridge ever existed.

"She said the state damned up the water way feeding the creek about thirty-five years ago. Then, when the interstates were built a new road was opened by-passing the bridge. As far as we know the Bowling Green Police Department may not know where the bridge is."

JW frowned for a few long seconds, then sighed, and slapped the flashlight against his thigh.

"I don't like it, but you're probably right," he said opening the car door. "You'd better get going. I hope Mona's okay."

"Yeah, me too," Preston whispered.

Once John Wayne was clear of the car Preston pressed on the gas pedal and moved slowly over the rough terrain. Parasitic kudzu vines consumed a large area of white oak and yellow pine trees, wrapping itself around the tree trunks, uprooting several, and smothering assorted weeds and bushes with a blanket of green death. If not for the tracks recently made by a car traveling through the vegetation he would have been lost.

The sweat stink of fear soaked his shirt. Puffing heavily, he pulled the shirt away from his neck with two fingers, shaking the fabric to try and cool the desperation away. It was taking much too long to get there, yet he didn't have any idea how far, or even where, the bridge could be. The anxiety made him want to puke.

He rolled the car window down and felt the brisk autumn night frost the wet shirt. It felt as cold as sitting in a tub of ice. Cold but good, until a blood curdling scream from somewhere in the thick dark forest shattered the stillness, turning the cold shirt collar into a tortuous garrote, closing around his neck, choking him as if one of those ice cubes was being shoved down his throat.

Chapter 22

The weathered boards on the old covered bridge looked like broken teeth in the yawning mouth of a prehistoric beast. Most of the roof had disappeared from neglect long ago. The dilapidated structure was a disintegrating skeleton, a fossil of a time when neighbors pooled their money and energy to build a bridge needed to traverse the raging waters on horseback, wagons, and the occasional automobile. A time when the bridge with the strong roof on top was a prideful sight to behold.

Now the once grand edifice sat abandoned, crossing a usually dry creek bed. The water that once ran deep and full of fish was long ago dammed and rerouted. The road that once ran from the Franklin Road was closed when a new modern highway directed traffic away, and to the south. Vegetation now filled the cracks in the broken asphalt, spreading it apart, pushing all evidence of humanity aside.

In the flapper days of the 1920's gawkers used to come to the bridge, and park along the side of the road, taking pictures of the infamous covered bridge where the young college girl was hanged. Sometimes they would bring food and have picnics on the spot where the local newspaper said she was tied, raped and beaten before finally being murdered. By the end of the Great Depression years of the 1930's very few people even knew a girl had died here. People had little time, or money, to spend on stories about a dead girl. They were too busy trying to survive themselves.

Then, in 1955, word began spreading across the Western Kentucky College campus that the ghost of a young woman was haunting the old covered bridge out near the Franklin Road. According to the legend, the girl had been raped and murdered by a carload of thugs, who, when they had finished with her, hung her body off the bridge. The story said the ghost would first appear in the form of a small blue light rising from under the bridge. Then it would grow larger and brighter as it came out of the creek bed, finally transforming into the shape of a beautiful woman with a rope dangling from her neck. She was forever seeking revenge against her killers.

Word spread like wildfire, and the ghost girl became the hottest topic around fraternity campfires. For a brief period, a new make out destination was born.

Cuddle up, drink some beer, do a little lovin', see a ghost, and enjoy a cheap night of thrilling entertainment.

But, as with everything else in life all good things come to an end. By 1965 the ghost girl was only a memory to a few old timers who even remembered there ever was a covered bridge, much less a vengeful ghost.

The real murdered girl was only remembered in police files.

Chapter 23

Fog was gathering around the bridge like a mist filled moat when Julie Cramer pulled the blue Ford to a stop. She turned off the engine and closed her eyes, while images of hideously terrible things flashed in slow motion across her mind. She shivered, and blinked angrily, trying to make the hateful mental movie projector go away.

Willing the image to dissolve, she sat staring bleakly at the gaping jaws of the desolate site of horror for several minutes, tears filling her eyes. She dabbed at her cheeks with a tissue and wiped her nose.

"So much pain," she cried. "So much hurt."

She blew her nose and tossed the wet tissue on the floorboard. She looked back at Mona Cooper lying helplessly on the back seat and sneered.

"You still sleepin' Lady Mona? Would you like me to run a hot bath for your Ladyship?" she laughed mirthlessly. "I wonder what Freddy Desmond would think of you now. Freddy Desmond didn't date ugly girls, and you're ugly. In fact, you're so ugly you look like you've been in a dog fight.

"Oh, wait a minute, is that my fault? Humph! Now I guess you'll complain it wasn't fair for me to hit you with your hands tied behind your back. Well, that's just too damn bad, Sister! It wasn't fair for Freddy Desmond to hang me off that damn bridge either!"

Mona moaned. The position she'd been shoved into was almost unbearable. Every muscle in her body ached. She twisted around trying to find some semblance of comfort and kicked the front seat behind Julie Cramer. Cramer growled angrily and reached back over the seat and ripped off the grey duct tape covering Mona's mouth. With a savage cry, she hit Mona violently across the face with the side of her fist, giggling when Mona's head bounced against the seat.

"Don't move again," she hissed.

Mona whimpered quietly and adjusted herself against the back of the seat. "Why are you doing this?" she said her voice trembling. "Where are we?"

"We are where it all began," Julie Cramer said in a dull monotone, her eyes staring into the past.

"I don't understand."

"Oh, don't play dumb with me...you...stupid slut! You know where it started."

Mona barely moved her head, struggling to rise. "I really don't know what you're talking about."

"You really are stupid, aren't you?"

"Where are we, Julie?"

Being called Julie scalded Cramer like Mona had thrown boiling water in her face. She screeched a loud piercing wail and swung her arm back over the seat striking Mona across the face with her forearm. The cartilage in Mona's nose popped with a sickening crunch sending blood running down her cheeks. Too weak to scream, Mona merely groaned, her head pounding with each heartbeat.

"*My name is Karen! Karen O'Day! Karen O'Day!*" Cramer screamed, the veins in her temples swelling with rage. "Don't you *ever* call me that name again. Do you understand? If you ever call me that name again, I will make you beg me to kill you! Is that clear enough for you, Bitch! Now lay down and shut up. I've got to think."

"I'm sorry...Karen, I'm sorry..."

"I said shut up!"

Despite the Ford's huge back seat Mona could barely move. She whimpered as quietly as possible as spasms attacked her back and cramped her leg muscles. Her back ached, spreading from the top of her neck to her tailbone, throbbing like a toothache. Both rotator cuffs burned, twisted and torn, shooting excruciating needles of pain like electric charges racing down both arms. Tears, mingled with the blood on her face, exposing the hopelessness growing inside her. She shifted her body several times unable to control the tremors.

"I swear, Cooper. If you move one more time, I'm going to crush your skull with a rock."

Mona closed her eyes and prayed that O'Day couldn't feel the body tremors making the seat pulsate with each beat of her heart. She shook all over when Karen O'Day opened the car door and got out. Unable to see what was happening outside the car, fear caused her to pass out.

The night was pitch black when Karen walked to the edge of the bridge. She knelt, scouring underneath with a penetrating gaze, but in the dark she was unable to get a satisfying view. She rose and moved into the creek bed.

The bridge had seen rain sometime during the day and the creek stones were slippery. She slipped and fell, catching herself with her right hand, twisting her wrist. She scowled and rubbed the ache. Cursing, she rose and continued walking, this time more slowly.

Two steps later she tripped again, grimacing in pain when her knee landed on a stone the size of her fist. She grabbed the rock and threw it savagely at the hated structure. The stone hit with a solid thud and another board dropped with a crash to the ground. As soon as the rotten timber hit the mud Karen's head jolted up like a marionette on a string.

"What…*What*!" she shouted her eyes wild with anger, her head jerking robotically like a windup toy. "Who are you? *Who are you?*" she demanded. "Where are you, damn it!" As if following a silent command her eyes flicked to the black gaping mouth of the bridge. "Is that you, Freddy? What do you want? What? Why? Why do I have to kill her?"

Her shoulders dropped as she blindly felt her way through the dark to the edge of the river. Trembling like a battered puppy she eased down on the bank. "Freddy, no!" she said shaking her head violently. "The new Freddy was supposed to kill her. What? No…no…no, I told him to take care of her! He's supposed to do it! That's why I brought her here!"

Her head suddenly jerked sideway as if struck by an unseen fist. She screamed in pain, caressing her face with both hands as she lowered her head in surrender.

"Please, don't hurt me again, Freddy, please. I've never killed anyone." She sat quietly rubbing her cheek for several minutes, afraid to move, then she slowly raised her defeated eyes to the ghoulish yawning mouth of the bridge and nodded. "Okay, if that's what you want." Breathing a sigh of despair, she pushed to her feet and stumbled to the car.

I don't want to do this, she thought. As she opened the trunk, she took a deep breath and grabbed the hemp rope lying atop the spare tire. She slammed the lid shut, and with a resigned sigh threw her shoulders back, went to the rear passenger door, and yanked the door open.

The sight of Mona Cooper lying unconscious on the back seat, like a calf awaiting slaughter, flipped a toggle switch in Karen's brain. In the blink of a pus-filled eye the fleeting feeling of compassion soured into unadulterated hate. Mona was the bitch standing between her and the sweet delicious taste of revenge she craved. In one quick motion she lassoed the end of the rope around Mona's ankles and jerked with all her might.

The touch of rope pressing against her skin stirred Mona awake. She screamed in panic kicking straight out catching Karen in the middle of the stomach. Karen doubled over gasping for breath. The kick added to the rage of a rabid dog, and Karen shrieked like a banshee, yanking the rope as hard as she could. Mona flopped out the door like the seat had been waxed, bashing her head against the door frame. Blood spurted on the side of the car and down her head. Stunned, and with both hands tied behind her, Mona hit the ground flat with a thud.

Karen clasped her blood-soaked hands over her head laughing triumphantly and danced around Mona like a prize fighter who'd just won the fight. She made several turns around her victim, and then stopped, staring with empty eyes at the defenseless woman. Then, empathetic as a camp guard at Auschwitz, she kicked Mona in the ribs. Mona quivered, too weak to moan.

Karen grunted a pitiless chuckle and nudged the motionless figure with her foot. Seeing no sign of movement, she walked to the creek's edge, picked up a stone the size of a football, and carried it back to the car. In one cold calm motion, she raised the rock straight up with both hands and smashed it down on the side of Mona Coopers head, twice, cracking her skull like a melon.

Karen folded cross-legged on the wet ground next to Mona, watching her for several minutes. When Mona no longer twitched, she rose to her knees, grabbed a handful of Mona's hair, lifted her head, and placed two fingers against her throat. A faint pulse, hardly perceptible, fluttered in the carotid artery. Smiling grimly, she removed the rope from Mona's ankles, formed a circle with a slipknot, and looped the rope over Mona's head.

Not convinced she'd done enough she stood up, and, with an animalistic roar, stomped down on Mona's chest, feeling the ribcage cave in under her feet. A burst of air shot from Mona's ruptured lungs. With a vicious yank she pulled the knot tight around the unconscious woman's neck

Karen cursed as she struggled to wrap the long rope over her own shoulders and around her waist creating a crude harness. Finally fitted, she took a deep breath and leaned against the weight of Mona's body. Pulling a hundred and twenty pounds of dead weight over rocky mud was harder than she expected. She had to stop every few steps to catch her breath.

With sweat running down her face in the unusually cold October night, she finally reached the edge of the creek. Mona's face was twisted and distorted, her skin a blackish hue, her lips swollen, bluish-red, and meaty. Karen reached down and checked for a pulse.

"Freddy made me do it, Mona," She growled and shrugged without feeling.

She dragged the limp body to the banks edge and pushed hard until it rolled over the rim like a big bag of potatoes. The body move two feet and stopped.

Cursing, she stumbled down the incline, dropped to her seat, and using her legs shoved Mona the rest of the way down the slope. Mona came to rest in a lump under the bridge.

Nearly exhausted, Karen stood gasping for air, hands on her hips, feet shoulder width apart like a psychotic version of *Wonder Woman*. After several minutes, partially recovered, she walked under the bridge, picked up the end of the rope, and with a weary heave tossed it over the same crossbeam that was used in 1920.

A sudden crash echoing through the forest brought her up short. She dropped the rope across Mona's torso, jumped behind the corner of the bridge and peered intently into the darkness.

Chapter 24

Going too slow, going too slow!!!! Oh God!!! Going too slow!!!
Preston Desmond stomped hard on the accelerator. The vette jumped forward for about twenty feet, and then as if sucked into a black hole, the front end dropped forward and down, slamming nose first into a crater four to five feet deep. The edge of the fissure, acting as a fulcrum under the belly of the car, crumbled into clumps of clay as the back wheels swung completely off the ground, leaving the Corvette teetering back and forth like a seesaw on a playground.

Frustrated tears mixed with heartbreaking worry ran down his cheeks as he edged out of the suspended vehicle. He placed one foot on the crust of the crater, and slowly shifted sideways on the seat easing out the door. As he twisted into position to jump out of the car, the vehicle lurched forward, throwing him face first against the window frame splitting his upper lip, and hitting his front teeth. A sharp pain, like red hot lightning ignited his jaws, and then quickly spread into a dull pulsating ache.

He grimaced and slapped both hands over his mouth to muffle the cries about to explode. Shaking with pain fueled anger, he cursed silently, spat out a glob of blood, and checked to see if his front teeth were still in place. His pain was jarringly thrown aside when Julie Cramer's angry screams echoed through the forest.

Ignoring the pain in his mouth and powered by panic driven adrenaline he scrambled on his belly through the weeds until he was safely away from the sink hole. Once on solid ground he jumped to his feet and hurried in the direction his instincts told him the screams came from.

He kept to the side of the road for about a hundred yards, cringing with each twig snapping under his feet, each sound echoing in his brain like a snare drum rim shot. Time, space and distance melded together, like the past, present and future were happening at once. How far back to the main road? How far to the creek? Is Mona still alive. Every ounce of his being cried out it's too late, every beat of his heart prayed it wasn't.

And then suddenly he detected the sweet familiar whiff in the wind. A hint of a flower wafting through the trees. An aroma not yet in season. A trace of lilacs and roses, the intoxicating fragrance always with her; the calling card of

Karen O'Day or Julie Cramer, or whoever the hell she was. It was her magic spell, her Charlotte's web.

My God, she must have cases of that damn perfume, he thought. Crouching like a lion stalking prey, he crept forward silently, quietly, eyes alert and determined.

The road suddenly veered left. Through the trees he heard her talking to herself. He stopped and listened, slowly inching forward.

Then in the moonlight he saw her under the bridge, standing like an executioner with rope in hand.

"Hello, Preston?" she said with a false sweetness. "Darling, you should know by now that you can't hide from me. I heard you sneaking through the woods like Natty Bumppo." She laughed loudly. "Believe me, dear. You are not the Deer Slayer."

Surprise gone he stepped out into the open. He knew Karen was under the bridge, but he didn't see Mona.

Maybe she's okay, he thought. The hope that Mona was alive sent his heart racing. Hope crumbled into despair when he saw her bloody body lying under the bridge. Retching dry heaves, he staggered sideways nearly dropping to his knees.

"Oh, Karen…why?"

"Why indeed?" Karen said, chuckling a strange guttural sound, her eyes shifting to where he stood. "You thought you were going to sneak in and save little Mona, didn't you, Natty?" She grunted and sucked her teeth loudly. "Well, I'm sorry to tell you this, darling. But you're about five minutes too late."

"Why…Karen, what are you doing?"

"I'm hanging the bitch, what does it look like?" she shouted. She paused, and then added in an ominous tone "I'm hanging her the same way you hanged me, Freddy."

"Damn it!" Preston shouted. Then fighting to keep his voice calm he took several deep breaths, and in a soft pleading voice said, "Karen…you know I'm not Freddy." He moved slowly toward the bridge, inches at a time, hoping to get between her and Mona before she could stop him. "In your heart you know it wasn't me that killed your aunt."

"It was me you bastard!" She screamed an ear-splitting shriek. Chills shuddered through him like waves of silverfish swimming under his skin. "It was me you murdered! Me! You murdered me, not my stupid aunt. Oh, it was me, you *son of a bitch!*"

Tears filled her eyes overflowing into ragged streams of mascara running down her face. Her voice dropped to a doggish growl, her lips twisting red and grotesque.

"You killed me, Freddy. It was you! Oh, how I've waited for this day."

"But why Mona? She's never done anything to you---"

"Shut up!" she screamed. Her bloodshot eyes caught his in a grip that seemed to come straight from the pits of hell. Then, in an instant, they softened, and she appeared to get lost in the past, her voice becoming dreamy, mesmerizing, hypnotic.

"Do you remember that night, Freddy? It was very foggy, kind of like tonight, when you brought me here, remember? But that's why you asked Felix Curtis to pick me up after cheerleading practice, wasn't it? You were supposed to pick me up, weren't you?

"You know, at the time I wondered why you had him do that, but later it became so obvious. I was even more surprised when you had him take me all the way out to Beach Bend Park." She chuckled, and a hint of a smirk touched her lips as she peered back into another time and place. The minute journey into the past grew hard when her stone-cold eyes met his. "To show you how dumb, and how much in love I was, I really did think we were going to a nightclub to celebrate our upcoming engagement. Wow!" she chuckled with a sneering shake of her head. "How wrong could I have been.

"I always knew you were smart, smarter than all of us put together, but I didn't realize until it was too late just how stupid I was. You planned it so carefully, and Felix was the perfect patsy, same height, same build, same weight, even the same hair color." She paused and wiped away the tears with the back of her hand.

"Oh God," she whispered. "In the fog, no one could tell the two of you apart." She chuckled scornfully. "But the real stroke of genius was the fact that if it had not been foggy, everyone would have seen Felix with me. It was so perfect."

As she talked, reliving the past, Preston inched closer to Mona.

"I've read all the transcripts, Freddy," she continued. "During the trial, Felix tried to tell them he delivered me to you, that he was doing you a favor, at your request. But no one would believe him. No one could believe that the marvelous Frederick Desmond would do such a heinous thing to the woman he loved." A razor-sharp glare cut into Preston. "But you didn't really love me, did you? I don't think you're even capable of love."

"Karen," Preston said softly, moving closer to Mona. "If I am, as you say, the reincarnation of Freddy Desmond, then why aren't you taking it out on me? Why are you hurting Mona?"

Karen's face softened into a complexed Mona Lisa smile. "Because, I love you, Freddy. And, I hate you. I loved you for what we had, and I hate you for what you did. But now I'm with you again, and I always will be. I will never leave you, Freddy."

Her words left him weak. He shivered as he said, "That doesn't explain why you're doing this to Mona."

Karen shook her head in frustration. "You still don't get it, do you? You still don't believe me."

Still edging closer, he slid his right foot side-ways, and tripped over a dead branch hidden by the brush. Staggering forward, his momentum threw him against a large tree stump with a loud *umph*!

Karen's eyes tightened into slits. She jerked the rope, twisting Mona's head in a deadly angle.

"You move another step, and I'll pull her head off. Now, shut up and listen. I'm going to tell you exactly what happened that night. No one knows but Freddy and me. I'm sure you'll remember." Her angry eyes met his like crossed swords.

Preston raised both hands. "Okay, I'm…I'm listening…just don't hurt her anymore."

"Humph, it's a little too late to worry about that." Karen grunted, and glanced angrily at Mona, but didn't do anything. After a moment she looked back at him and said, "Sit down, Freddy."

"I don't want---"

"I said sit down!" She ordered, staring hypnotically until he dropped Indian style to the ground.

"That's better." Still holding tightly to the rope, she moved to a large boulder growing out of the creek bank and eased down. "When Felix Curtis pulled into the park's entrance, instead of parking in front he drove all the way around to the rear of the maintenance building. At that time, I still thought we were going to the *Blind Tiger* speakeasy in Glasgow. Of course, we now know that was never your plan.

"You were waiting in your car. I got out of Felix's car and joined you, and he drove away." She grunted, shaking her head. "Poor Felix. The fool had no idea…

"Any way, when I asked you why all the sleight of hand with Felix, and why you were hiding at the park, you just laughed and said you had a surprise for me. I asked what it was, and you said I couldn't see it until we got there.

"That's when you put the blindfold on me. Now Freddy, that scared me. You'd never done anything like that before. But you said you loved me, and for me to trust you. So, I relaxed, and as we drove, we talked about what we were going to do after graduation, and who we would invite to the wedding, and how wonderful our life would be once we were married and had a family."

Her eyes returned from the far away and met Preston's with a wistful smile touching her lips, like seeing a long-lost photograph.

"It seemed like we drove for hours. Of course, cars didn't go very fast in those days, and I'm sure it was probably a much shorter time than it felt." She paused and took a breath. "Finally, we turned off the main road. With the blindfold on I could tell the road wasn't traveled very much because it was so incredibly bumpy. I mean it was very bumpy. At one point you reached over and patted me on the leg, so gently, so sweetly."

The smile began to fade, and her voice took on a sad raspy tone. "Then we came to a stop, and I could smell the fishy mineral smell of the creek. There had been a lot of rain, and I could hear water splashing against something. I realized later it was the bridge supports. That's when you changed."

"Karen---"

Her hand shot up pointing a warning finger at Preston. He closed his mouth.

"You jerked the blindfold off of me very roughly," she said, "and you grabbed my blouse tearing several buttons away. I was shocked, I couldn't speak, I didn't know what was happening, my mind raced, and I could feel my heart pounding in my chest. Something was wrong, but I couldn't understand what it was."

As she spoke, the pictures were so clear Preston could see it all in his mind. It was like he was there:

Karen was crying. Her face cupped in her hands; her shoulders racked by sobs. She was pleading with Frederick Desmond who stood with his back to her, arms folded across his chest, feet planted firmly on the ground. Karen ran to him, and threw her arms around him, desperately pressing her face against his back. Instead of holding her, Desmond whipped around violently, lashing out with both fists.

Preston closed his eyes, hoping desperately to clear his mind of the images she so vividly painted of the muscular All-American Freddy Desmond savagely beating the helpless young woman. Guttural sobs emerged from Preston's throat as his mind's eye saw the iron fists mercilessly smashing into the beautiful girl. The more she implored, the more she begged, the more she cried the harder he hit her. She couldn't take much more, but on it went, until finally Freddy Desmond's arms got tired. He grabbed her by the front of the blouse and lifted her off the ground.

"Whose baby is it? You, stupid, filthy bitch!" He hit her across the face with the back of his hand. "I've been too careful!" He hit her again.

Karen, weak from the blows could only mumble incoherently.

"I saw you with Felix Curtis, you slut…I saw you!" All she could do was shake her head, no, it wasn't true. She tried to loosen the grip he had on her, but her hands and arms were too weak, and they dropped to her side.

"No bitch is going to trap me," he yelled, throwing her to the ground. He stood glaring down at her, his left hand unbuckling his belt. "You want a baby, huh? I'll give you a baby!"

Her screams sent shock waves through Preston. He tried to shut them out, pressing his hands tight against his ears. The cries only intensified. They were in his head.

"Then you reached under my skirt," Karen said, "and tore off my panties."

Preston closed his eyes. All he could see was his grandfather brutally raping Karen O'Day on the cold muddy ground. He cried out, trying to erase the imagery in his head but it didn't work.

His mind's eye watched as Freddy Desmond pushed himself off Karen and pressed his face close to her ear.

"I've got too many plans," he said. "Too many plans, and none of them include you." Then, from nowhere, a rope appeared in his hand. "You almost ruined everything, Karen. My God! How could you do this to me?" As he said the words that were destroying her heart, his hands were looping the rope that would end her life. Preston cried out in horror as his mind's eye watched Freddy Desmond slip the knot over Karen's head, and strangle her.

When Karen stopped moving Desmond dragged her down to the creek bank. Standing waist deep in the water he ran one end of the rope over a bridge support and hauled the unconscious body up until her feet washed back and forth with the currents.

He pulled Felix Curtis' student ID from his shirt pocket with his thumb and index finger, wiped the fingerprints off with his shirttail, and holding it with the shirt casually tossed the card on the muddy ground. With a quick downward thrust he ripped the pocket off a shirt he'd brought with him, shredded a small piece, and jammed it under the middle fingernail of Karen's right hand.

The force was so great it tore the fingernail partially off her finger. A small trickle of blood oozed from the torn nail. He reached up and pulled the noose tighter around Karen's neck.

Preston could hardly breathe as he watched Fredrick Desmond shift into a boxer's stance, and then brutally punch Karen O'Day in the stomach.

Repulsed yet hypnotically absorbed in the story she so graphically painted he didn't realize she had slipped behind him, until a crashing blow to the back of his head turned everything black.

Chapter 25

Consciousness returned in a kaleidoscopic display of bright, multicolored lights, cavorting through a head that felt like it had been split with an axe. He tried to massage his hammering temples but found his hands wouldn't move. It hurt to swallow, and his shirt collar felt like an under-size dog collar. His parched mouth tasted like dead fish were rotting on his tongue.

He started to open his eyes, but before he could move something hard and rough as a tree limb hit him in the face. He groaned.

"Wake up, Freddy Desmond! I don't have all night," a hoarse, gravely, voice yelled with a cackling laugh. "Hey, wait a minute! Yes, I do!"

Preston Desmond was conscious enough to know he was on his back, and his hands were tied behind him. He let his head loll over to the left. Karen O'Day was straddling a large boulder nonchalantly slapping one end of a rope against the side of the rock, the other end was tied around his neck. She laughed and yanked the rope hard a couple of times lifting his head up off the ground.

"Not so much fun when you're on the receiving end is it, Freddy?" She pulled the rope two more times causing Preston to growl a choking gagging gasp. Giggling like a school girl at a slumber party, she yanked again, harder this time. "Quit being such a wuss…cause baby, you ain't seen nothin' yet."

Preston tasted thick bloody bile filling his mouth. He tried to force-swallow against the tight thick rope but couldn't. Twisting his body around he managed to roll over onto his side, open his mouth, and let the putrid mess slide out onto the ground.

"Where's Mona?" he rasped.

"You've got more to worry about than that miserable thing."

"Where is she, Karen? Where is Mona?"

Karen shrugged nonchalantly and instead of answering, began to sing. "*Somewhere, over the rainbow*…no, that's not right. Oh, wait, now I remember," she said pointing toward the bridge. "I kicked her over the bank into the creek over there." She tilted her head childlike, closed her eyes, and in a sing-song voice said, "*Roses are red violets are blue, I think she be dead, and soon so will you.*"

She twisted her cracked lips tightly and scrunched up her nose, as if smelling something rotten. "If she's not dead, she sure is ugly."

"So now you're going to kill me?"

"Of course, I am, Freddy," she said matter-of-factly. "That's been the plan since the night I saw you on TV and found out you were in Bowling Green. You know what they say, murderers always return to the scene of the crime. Well, you certainly did. And now you have to pay for killing me." She paused when a shadow of sadness fell across her eyes. "I thought it would be easier for me to kill you than it is. It's not. You know why?"

He mumbled, "Why?"

"Because, I found out I still love you." She gave her head a quick shake and the sadness in her eyes vanished. "But you hurt me so bad. I hate you for that, you bastard."

"Okay, so now you hate me. What does that have to do with Mona? Why did you have to hurt her?"

"Mona was bait darling. It got you here," she said. She snickered, and with an apathetic shrug, said, "To tell you the truth, I just don't like the bossy slug." She adjusted herself on the rock and stretched her legs out in front of her. She sat staring into space for several long minutes, then let out a deep resigned sigh. "Well, Freddy my love, it's time for you to begin your journey to hell. Get up!"

"I can't, my hands are tied."

"You're a strong boy, stand up!"

"Karen, if you think I'm going to help you kill me, you're crazier than I thought you were. *You* can go to hell!"

"Oh, I'm sure I will. But not right now. Now, get up!"

"Can't do it, *Julie!*"

A red veil of hate swept over O'Day's face, the swollen veins pulsating like engorged earthworms. She sat frozen to the spot, beating the sides of her thighs with clenched white-knuckle fist, her jaw muscles dancing a minuet.

"Okay!" she screamed, "I'll choke you right here!"

She whirled her legs around to the back of the boulder, stood up, and placed one foot on the side of the rock. Adjusting her feet for leverage, she yanked the rope as hard as she could. Preston gasped a gurgling cry as the cord tightened deeper around his throat. The knot forced the blood gorging into his face, turning the stretched skin a grisly reddish blue.

He flopped spastically across the ground like a fish fighting a hook, his bloodshot eyes bulging out like a bullfrog's. Then slowly, the spasms stopped, his eyelids quivered faintly, then closed.

Karen stood for several heartbeats watching Preston's body. When his chest vaguely moved, she dropped the rope and eased close to the motionless form.

Preston Desmond is a big, strong man, she thought, *he might be faking it. It's better to be safe than sorry. That's what my mama always said.*

She knelt on one knee and cautiously placed two fingers against his carotid artery. A faint pulse brought a self-satisfied smirk.

"You better not die yet, you son of a bitch."

She reached over, and, with the edge of her hand, rabbit punched him in the solar plexus. The blow sent a gob of red foamy spit shooting out his mouth onto her arm.

"Ewww…You…gross son-of-a-bitch! You're disgusting!"

She wiped her arm on his chest and picked up the rope. She was halfway to her feet when the cracking sound of something, or someone, stepping on dry brush broke the silence. Her ears pricked up.

"Who's there?" she growled, her eyes scanning the forest, her head oscillating from left to right like a weathervane in a cross wind.

"*Julie Cramer,* this is the Bowling Green Police!" a megaphoned voice called from the forest.

Karen's head shook violently. "No, you are not! There's no one here."

"Miss Cramer, this is Detective Jim Watkins. Drop the rope!"

"You're not really here. You've never been here! You weren't here then…" Her voice sounded strange, distant.

"Miss Cramer drop the rope now, and move away from Preston Desmond," Watkins said. Four uniformed police officers, guns locked and loaded, made their way out of the trees surrounding the bridge.

"Humm…woo…" Karen hummed softly as if in a dream.

"Julie, drop the rope now."

Tears began running down her face, she looked up toward the covered bridge and let out a shuddering sigh. The low, terrible, distressful moan sent chills running up the detective's arms.

"Julie," he said gently. "Please, we don't want to hurt you. Drop the rope and get down on your knees."

Karen O'Day's tormented eyes met his. "Detective why weren't you here when *I* needed you? Why weren't you here…"

She expelled a deep sad sigh, shook her head, and with a last bloodcurdling scream, twisted the rope wrapped around Preston's neck and leaped off the rock toward the bridge.

Multiple shots rang out and Karen O'Day's body crashed face first on the rocks.

Chapter 26

Voices outside the hospital room woke Preston Desmond from a restless sleep. After four days lying on his back, being prodded, pricked and probed, he was ready to go home. His throat didn't feel as sore as he thought it would, but the purple bruises on his neck had a long way to go before they were gone. The deep gash on his head required twelve stitches, but other than having a mild concussion, the doctors didn't think there was any damage done to his brain. Other than that, his whole body was tender to the touch.

A faint knock on the door stirred him alert. After a few seconds Detective James Watkins walked in smiling broadly, a toothpick sticking out of the corner of his mouth.

"How you are feeling Preston?" he said, reaching out to shake Preston's hand. He removed the little wooden stick from his mouth and slipped it in his coat pocket.

"I feel a lot better," Preston said slipping his hands under the sheet and massaging the knuckles on his right hand. Watkin's handshake felt like a vise-grip on the swollen fingers. "My mother was in earlier," he said. "She told me they had to put Mona in a coma. She said the doctor believes that despite the torture Mona suffered she's going to make it. She's going to survive."

The crow's feet on the detective's eyes sprang upward. He placed his hand on Preston's shoulder, and gently squeezed.

"That is absolutely amazing," he said. "No…it's a full fledge miracle." He paused and pulled a notebook from his coat pocket. "The report I read, I took some notes," he said tapping on the tablet. "The report said Mona's skull was fractured in two places, that she has a severe concussion, two broken vertebras in her neck, three broken ribs, a perforated lung, and a ruptured spleen. It's unbelievable that she survived." He lifted his eyes to Preston. "Did you know she was DOA, dead on arrival, when she was brought in."

"No, I didn't," Preston mouthed, fighting back the tears.

There was an awkward silence before Watkins said, "Have you been told about Julie Cramer?"

The mention of Julie Cramer's name was met with a blank stare. Preston shrugged indifferently despite the parade of goose bumps marching up his back.

"Detective, I've been out of it most of the time. I don't remember much about that night. No one has told me anything."

Watkins nodded his understanding.

"Okay, let me tell you what's been going on." He moved a chair close to the bed and sat down. "To cut to the chase, you and Mona Cooper won't have to worry about that troubled woman again. Julie Cramer died on the operating table, Saturday night, at 10:45 pm. The amazing coincidence is that at 10:47 pm, Mona's doctor realized she was alive and recorded the time on her chart." He chuckled. "Now that's what I call poetic justice."

"That's what I call weird," Preston said, suddenly feeling strangely uneasy. He picked up the cup of water off the bed tray, took a sip, and set the cup back down. "Detective Watkins, do you believe in reincarnation?"

Watkins laughed. "No, Preston, I don't. I believe once you're gone, you're gone. What brought that up?"

"Well, I've been lying here, thinking about Karen…or Julie, or whoever, and I don't know what to believe. I mean after all the things we went through, and the way she told me what happened; I mean…I mean, I could see everything happening in front of me, like I was there…I could see it!

"Only someone who was there could know that much about what happened in that much detail."

"Preston, she made all that crap up. She could have described any kind of scenario and made it sound real. There's no way to could prove or disprove any of it. The woman was a mental case."

"You do know that Karen O'Day was Julie Cramer's aunt, don't you?"

"Yes, but so what? That proves nothing. Answer me this. How much do you know about Frederick Desmond, or your great aunt on your mother's side, or… oh, I don't know, any of your ancestors? I would venture to say very little. All any of us really know about our kinfolks are the bits and pieces we hear at family reunions and sitting around the kitchen table."

"That's true," Preston admitted.

Detective Watkins smiled empathically and nodded. "You know as well as I do, Preston, life moves on, everything changes, and as people die, their sad, funny, and somewhat interesting stories die with them, replaced by new stories told by the living. This carnival that we call life is on a stop and go track leading to parts unknown."

"I understand all of that," Preston said, and then with puzzled look, said, "What does it have to do with Julie Cramer or Karen O'Day, or whatever name she used?"

"Only this, Julie Cramer was mentally ill. She was a psychopathic con-artist who could make things up on the fly. She saw you somewhere, who knows where, and became obsessed with you. In her obsession she created an entirely make-believe world based on a few pictures of people who resembled each other." He paused and looked at his watch. "A lot of what she created started when she was a student on the hill with Professor Jones. He messed her life up in more ways than one."

Watkins looked at his watch again and tapped the side of the bed. "I'd better get out of here and let you rest." He rose to his feet and grinned. "Got a little police business to take care of. I just wanted to stop by and see how you're doing."

"I'm glad you came in, Detective."

"Hey, call me Jim," Watkins said with a grin. He slapped Preston lightly on the side of the leg. "Take care of yourself, son."

After the detective was gone Preston lay staring out the window watching the water-filled clouds block out the sun. His heart felt heavy. The life he and Mona planned together would probably never happen. The physical and psychological trauma Mona suffered would probably be more than she could ever overcome.

Troubled by the future he stared blankly at the ceiling until sleep ushered in unwanted dreams.

Epilogue

Nashville, Tennessee – November 10, 1965

Word the doctors were reducing the anesthetics keeping Mona Cooper in a coma traveled fast. Almost immediately the waiting room at Vanderbilt Medical Center was standing room only. Relatives, sorority sisters, cheerleading teammates, and other friends anxious to see her filled the room, with several left standing in the hallway.

The prevailing question on everyone's mind, what condition would Mona be in. Would she be a cripple? The violence inflicted on her body was catastrophic. Would her mind be irreparably destroyed? Many terribly damaged victims never fully recovered.

Or will she be locked in this horrible limbo forever attached to a machine. Anxiety was palpable throughout the room.

Oscar Wakefield, the minister at Mona's church, walked in, and, after visiting a moment with her parents, quietly asked the congregated to gather in a circle and pray for Mona. As if guided by an invisible force everyone shifted into position, and clasped hands. After a moment of silence, the preacher implored God to restore Mona Cooper to her lovely vibrant self.

When the prayer was finished the atmosphere in the waiting room felt like a funeral home chapel. No one moved for several minutes until Preston Desmond noticed Mona's tall, dark skinned, Pakistani doctor, his thick hair as white as his lab coat, walking down the hall. Every head in the room turned in unison as he hurried in.

He stopped just inside the door his hands tucked into his smock pockets. He scanned the room, located Mona's parents, George and Jenny Cooper, and went to them. George, a short, pot-bellied man with bushy eyebrows and a fringe of grey hair skirting a shiny dome, rose quickly to his feet. He shook the doctor's hand, and then stepped aside. Jenny sat quietly, only looking up at the doctor with tired, tear reddened, eyes. He smiled at Mrs. Cooper, and then looked around the room.

"Good Morning," he said without an accent. "I am Dr. Alex Kashmiri, Mona Cooper's physician. I'm very happy to tell you that Mona opened her eyes this morning. She was able to smile, although weakly, and surprisingly, even spoke a few words." Relief whooshed across the room like a ruptured compressed air tank.

Dr. Kashmiri cleared his throat and chuckled. "I should say Mona spoke about as well as a person can with a tube running down their throat."

Laughter, tears, and a few thank God's lifted the spirits of her family and friends.

"Doctor Kashmiri," John Wayne McKinney said quietly, "what exactly did you do, I mean I don't really understand any of it. I know she was in a coma, but…" he shrugged uncomfortably.

"That's a good question," the doctor said. "Your friend Mona was seriously injured. She's a strong woman, but I'm still very surprised she's alive." He paused and looked around the room. "Let me give a quick explanation of what took place.

"A medically induced coma is used to help patients recover from extremely serious injuries, particularly traumatic brain injuries. To induce a coma, we administer a cocktail of substances, including general anesthetic drugs, to patients in carefully controlled settings. The idea behind this treatment is to curtail the body's natural mechanisms, which would shut off blood flow to injured areas. By allowing blood to flow freely to the wound sites, medically induced comas support the healing process.

"Once the patient has shown that healing is taking place, we reduce the medication slowly, gently bringing them back to consciousness." He smiled again and looked at Jenny Cooper. "Mona responded extremely well. She is doing great."

Jenny Cooper let out a deep sigh, struggling to maintain control. "Thank you, Doctor. When can I see her?"

"You and Mr. Cooper can see her now. She'll probably look a little better to you than she has for the past couple of weeks, but don't expect too much. She's still not herself." He turned to Preston. "And you are her fiancé?"

"That's right," Preston said.

Kashmiri nodded. "I know she'll want to see you."

Jenny Cooper rose from the chair and was moving toward the door, when George Cooper gently caressed her arm and pulled her to him. He looked at Preston and nodded his head.

"Preston, why don't you go see her first, son. I know Mona would want to see you."

A surly grunt registered Jenny Cooper's discontent.

"Thank you, Mr. Cooper," Preston said.

He rushed from the room and ran down the hall, his heart hammering a mile a minute, pounding against his eardrums like the thump, thump, thump of a bass guitar. His temples throbbed from pressure building in his head.

With every step he tried to ease the tension building inside his body, to settle the nerves scrapping against his soul, to put on a happy front. But suddenly overcome with an unexplainable fear, he came to an abrupt stop outside her door.

He stood, he didn't know for how long, wiping the sweat running down his face with his shirttail, tears welling up in his eyes. His chest ached with guilt for every lie he ever told her, for every time he cheated, for every time he stood her up because he wanted to do something else. For all the selfish, egotistical, self-centered things he ever did. They all came rushing back, stabbing him like a thousand poisoned daggers gouging his heart, ripping his soul.

The bare truth finally dawned on him that he really did love her, and it shamed him to think it took nearly losing her to realize it. Tears ran unashamedly down his face. He wiped his eyes with both hands and pushed through the door.

Mona looked like a bruised, battered angel lying on a cloud of white, her head wrapped in gauze, tubes running in and out of her body. He walked to her bedside, gently took her hand in his, and kissed her softly on the cheek. Mona's eyelids fluttered briefly, and then edged open, a tender smile beginning to appear.

"I love you so much, Mona," Preston whispered.

The left side of Mona's mouth curled up thinly. "I...love...you too," she mouthed. Then closing her eyes, she breathed, "I'll never leave you, Freddy..."

Also, by Andy Weston

Now Available

In eBook and Paperback

VENGEANCE

A Beauregard Bell Investigation

Please turn the page for an exciting preview

It was one of those days when time moved slower than sap. I'd finished closing the books on a couple of accounts, and was about to tell my secretary, Desiree, that I was heading for the golf course when she appeared in front of my desk.

"Beau, a lady just came in who says she really needs to see you." Desiree looked at the note in her manicured hand. "Her name is Clair Canon."

"Clair?"

"She said she's an old friend." Desiree's full lips curled into a smile. "I'd say by your expression that she is."

I chuckled. "Clair and I go all the way back to the sixth grade, Desi. By the time we reached high school she was one of the most beautiful girls in the state. In fact, she was a runner up for Kentucky's Junior Miss our senior year.

"I don't think there was a boy who ever laid eyes on her that didn't get the hots for her. I was no different."

"Well, she's still attractive," Desiree said, "Maybe just a little too thick with the makeup, but attractive."

This was being said by a woman wearing designer Cleopatra eye makeup. I smiled at the irony.

"I haven't seen her in years," I said, "but the best I remember she wore very little makeup, just a little lipstick and a smidgen of eye shadow. Even without the paint Clair stood out from the crowd. She was voted homecoming queen two years in a row and was captain of the cheerleading squad. Hell, she was even the class valedictorian with a 4.0 GPA."

"It sounds like she was Miss Everything. How did you let her get away?"

"I tried to get her, believe me. But she was hung up on Jason Mire. He was the big man on campus...the big football star, you know the kind."

Desiree rolled her eyes. "I definitely know the kind. Correct me if I'm wrong. He had blonde hair, broad shoulders, and a Brad Pitt look. I'll bet he stood over six feet tall, didn't have an ounce of fat, and probably made straight A's; of course, ruining the grading curve for everyone else."

"Right on the money," I grunted. "Jason could have had any girl he wanted. No one else had a chance."

"She didn't know what she was passing up, did she?"

I shrugged. "She knew, but that's in the past. Jason is dead, and Clair is the wife of a United States Senator." I cleared the papers off my desk, and said, "Why don't you show her to my office?"

A few minutes later Clair Canon was standing at the door, a sheepish look on her face, an expensive blue suit on her trim body, and a small black purse in her hand. After pushing my initial admiration aside, I hurried to the door, took her hand, and escorted her to the leather chair in front of my desk.

"My lord, Clair, how long has it been, fifteen…sixteen years?"

"At least," she said.

"Well, you haven't changed a bit. You still look beautiful."

She smiled. "You wouldn't believe the amount of time and money I have to spend to look like this."

"Well, it's worth every penny."

She chuckled and straightened her skirt. "Thank you, but I think you lie. If I haven't changed, why did you have that questioning look in your eyes when I walked in? I distinctly recall how you used to look at me with those big brown eyes."

"That was a look of appreciation. You know I always looked at you appreciatively." With a touch of reluctance, I released her hand and went back to my chair. "What on earth are you doing so far from D.C., Clair? Visiting family?"

"Believe it or not I came to see you," she said glancing around the room nervously.

Before I continue, let me introduce myself. My name is Beauregard Bartholomew Bell III. I'm the junior partner of Beauregard Bell and Associates. We've been a full- service private investigations company since 1955. We have offices in 38 states and three countries. My grandfather founded the agency.

In 1980 Grandpa purchased a small chain of discount stores in North Carolina, and, by 1987, we had discount houses all over the country. That same year, Beauregard Bell Enterprises netted a little over 3 billion dollars. The business grew so fast and so big that in 1989 Gramps turned the reins of the investigative branch over to my Dad, BB Junior. 1989 was also the year I graduated from high school, which brings me back to Clair Canon.

"So, you came all this way just to see me?" I said interlocking my fingers behind my head and rocking back in the seat. "Now don't get me wrong, it's great to see you again, but I've been around the block too many times to believe this has anything to do with my irresistible charm."

"Don't sell yourself short, Beau," she said with a touch of flirtation. "The way I remember it, you did okay for yourself." She tilted her head raising one eyebrow. "I seemed to recall Vice-Principle Haden catching you and Claudine Maple on the wrestling mat behind the stage."

I laughed and held up my hands. "I plead innocent. We were practicing some holds."

"Oh, I'm sure you were." We both laughed and sat looking at each other for several moments. Finally, she took a deep breath, and let it out slowly. "Beau, I need your services."

I was quiet for several seconds studying her. She was more beautiful now than she was at twenty, even though her blonde hair was probably aided by Lady Clairol. She had put on a couple of pounds, but they were in the right places. Her waist was still trim and her skin smooth. Desiree had exaggerated about the makeup.

"I'm flattered, Clair. But surely the wife of a Senator has at least a dozen investigators to choose from."

"We do. My husband's law firm employ's several. But I wanted someone I knew I could trust." She paused, and her eyes met mine. "I don't want Randolph knowing what I'm doing."

"What are you involved in, Clair?"

She laughed. "Don't worry, it's nothing nefarious. It's just that he thinks I'm being paranoid."

"What gives him that idea?"

"It's because he gets this kind of stuff all the time. He's been in politics for over thirty years, and he's received every kind of correspondence you can think of, including threats. We've only been married for a couple of years, and I'm new to this. I've never had anyone threaten me before. It scares me. He thinks I'm making a mountain out of a mole hill."

"Someone is threatening you?" Suddenly very interested I leaned forward, resting my elbows on the desk.

"Yes," she said with a timid shrug. "At least I think so." With an almost apologetic smile, she glanced at her purse. It was a small black bag that appeared to have cost a young alligator its life. Clair Nathan had a reputation on animal rights that was almost as fanatical as the PETA nut cases. She caught me staring at the purse and chuckled. "It's faux alligator."

"I didn't have a doubt."

She smiled briefly, and then reached in the purse and pulled out an envelope about the size of a small greeting card. "Two months ago, I received this in the mail."

I noticed the card was addressed to Clair Canon, not Nathan. I slipped the note from the envelope.

God is jealous, and the Lord revenges.
The Lord will take vengeance
on his adversaries
and he reserves wrath for his enemies.
Nahum 1:2I

I read the note a couple of times and put it back in the envelope. "It's weird," I said, "but I wouldn't worry too much about it. This was probably some crackpot with nothing better to do?"

She shook her head. "If I'd only received the one, I don't think it would have bothered me, but I received a second."

She reached into her purse, retrieved another envelope, and handed it to me. Before opening it, I checked the postmark. The note was written on standard 20 weight paper and printed on a jet ink printer. It was mailed from East St. Louis, Illinois.

Behold, I come as a thief in the night…
Rev. 16:15

"What do you think?" she said nervously. "Should I be worried?"

"I think if I was your husband, I wouldn't have laughed it off."

"He didn't actually laugh it off. He thinks the notes were meant for him because of his stand on abortion. He's pro-abortion, and he's been getting a lot of hate mail from the pro-life crowd."

"But you don't agree?"

"No. The cards were addressed to Clair Canon, not Nathan…" She paused. "You don't think I'm being paranoid, do you?"

"No, I don't think this is a joke; but in most cases, a person who is going to do something very seldom sends a warning, much less two."

She leaned forward and placed a hand on the desk. "You really think so?"

"It is if you can believe statistics, and ten years investigating homicides for the Army CID."

She looked relieved as she moved a wayward strand of hair out of her eyes. "You have no idea how much better I feel."

She reached for the notes and I covered them with my hand

"Why don't you leave these with me? I want Punch Clayton to look at them."

"Okay."

I studied the stress lines in her face.

"Clair, let me ask you a question."

"Okay."

"It's been almost sixteen years since the last time we spoke. Why did you suddenly come all this way to show me a couple of flaky notes? A fax and a phone call would have accomplished the same thing? Do you know more about this than you're telling me?"

"What do you mean?" There was a slight shift in her body language.

"I mean the notes don't justify the trip."

"I told you I wanted someone I could trust."

"You could have taken them to the police. They would have kept an eye on you."

"I didn't think the police would help."

"What are you afraid of, Clair? Something prompted you to get on a plane and fly six hundred and fifty miles to see a man you haven't seen in over fifteen years."

"Well excuse me, Mr. Bell," she snapped rising from the chair. "You're the only detective I know. I thought you would help me. I must have been wrong. I'm sorry I wasted your time."

"Relax. I didn't say I wouldn't help you; and you're not wasting my time. Now smooth your feathers and sit down."

She glared at me for a couple of moments then sat back down.

"Clair, I do want to help you, but you've got to level with me. If you know anything, or even suspect something, or if you have any idea this is a personal thing, and not some off the wall wacko, I need to know about it."

I paused and watched her eyes. She met my gaze without a flinch.

"I don't have any idea who it could be."

"Well, as it is right now, the odds of me finding who sent these notes are about the same as you are winning the lottery...do you understand?"

She sighed and nodded.

"Good." I pulled a legal pad from the desk and reached for a pencil. "Now tell me a few things about you." I smiled reassuringly and looked in her green eyes. They were beginning to moisten.

"What do you want to know," she whispered.

"Well, for starters, who have you pissed off lately?"

She shook her head. "I can't think of anyone."

"What about ex-husbands?"

She looked down at her hands. "There was only one before Randolph. He died four years ago in a plane crash."

"What was his name?"

"You didn't know him."

"Humor me."

She sighed. "His name was Tommy Franklin."

I looked up from my note pad. "That wouldn't have been Tommy Franklin who owned the modeling agencies would it?"

"Yes, it was."

I grunted. "Umm, interesting…"

"Why?"

"I don't know. I thought he was…flamboyant. Wasn't he…? Uh, he had a reputation…"

Her lips tightened. "Is this really necessary?"

I placed the pencil on the desk and met her gaze. "Look, I'm not trying to drag up memories just for the hell of it. Whoever sent you the notes apparently has a grudge against you. Now if you want me to find out who it is, I need to know anyone who might have had a chip on their shoulder."

She was quiet for several seconds. Finally, she nodded.

"Tommy had several affairs, but I don't know if any of the people held grudges against me or not."

"If he was running around on you why did you stay?"

She stared defiantly in my eyes. When I showed as much emotion as King Tut's burial mask, she said, "For the money. I stayed with him for the money. Everybody doesn't grow up as rich as the Bell's. I allowed him his freedom, and he gave me carte blanche. It paid off. When he died, he left me the company, and twenty-eight million dollars. I sold the business for another fifty million."

I whistled under my breath. "I'd say that was a good reason to stay. It's also a good reason for someone to hate you. Did Tommy have any family, or any business associates that may have felt cheated?"

She shook her head. "None that I can think of…well, wait a minute, there is one person who felt slighted when the will was probated."

"Yeah, who's that?"

"Tommy's personal secretary."

"What's her name?"

A twisted smirk, faintly resembling a smile, formed on her lips. "His name is Delbert Martin."

I jotted the name on my note pad. "You think Delbert feels…mistreated?"

"You might say that. Delbert busted his ass for Tommy, and he received the same amount the other employees received."

"Which was?"

"Five thousand dollars…"

"And you ended up with seventy-eight million."

"Yes."

"Do you know where I can find Delbert Martin?"

"The last I heard he was living with Carlos Santorini, the fashion designer, in Miami."

I made a quick note to check Martin.

"What about you? Any old lovers that might be feeling spurned?"

She shook her head. "No."

"You're sure?"

"I'm very sure because there hasn't been any."

"None at all?"

"None!"

And so, it went. She felt threatened, and wanted me to protect her, but other than giving me the name Delbert Martin she was like the three monkeys who said nothing, saw nothing, and heard nothing. Still, the nagging feeling that she suspected more than she said kept eating at my gut.

Vengeance

Now Available

In eBook and Paperback

Available on eBook

The Clavis Isley Story

Shadow of the King

By Andy Weston

Green Cottage Publishing
P.O. Box 711
Fairdale, KY

PROLOGUE

Looking back most of it seems like a dream, and every year it gets harder to see the faces. They blur like the images on an old 1952 Philco television, just a fuzzy panorama of shadows rolling around in my mind. I don't even try to bring them into focus anymore there are just too many painful memories.

Cliff LaTorres is the only member of the band I've kept in touch with, but he's busy with the record company and nightclubs, so the visits are short. Still, he manages to stop by a couple times a month. His clubs are doing fabulously. You know he only books top name acts. The best! Of course, the club in Indianapolis is making the most money, but I guess when you consider the competition the one in Nashville has, it's not doing too shabbily.

I can still see Sara clearly, but that's only because I kept a couple of her pictures. I don't buy records and I watch very little television. Wasn't Thomas Wolfe the one who said you can never go home again? Well, it's true. This place is just a little wooden edifice with ghosts. Even the building is not original. The old farmhouse burned down. I rebuilt it pretty much the way it was, but it's different.

The old barn stood over where the garage is. When I was little, I used to play hide and seek in the loft with a neighborhood kid named Bill Skaggs and his sister Arabella. When I got older, I'd sneak my girlfriends up there and play other games. Almost got caught a couple of times.

That old barn, when the wind blew the sides would shake and whistle and carry on like the damn place was going to take off and fly. I don't know what kept it standing. And stink! Whew! I was always cleaning horseshit off my boots!

Did I tell you I was born here? Not in this house of course, like I said, it's a reconstruction, but on this spot. That was a lot of years ago. I was born on the day my daddy was shipped overseas. He never came back. When I was six months old mamma got a letter telling her that my daddy was killed somewhere in France.

That's what screwed her head up. I loved her, but she was usually off in another world. I don't mean to give you the idea she was a nut case because she wasn't. She just suffered from a deep depression. The doctors usually kept her medicated to the point she could barely function.

That left my upbringing to Pappy and Granny. Pappy was a wiry little man with strong hands and delicate features. He probably never weighed more than a hundred and thirty pounds in his life, but he was the hardest working person I ever met. He'd work sun-up to sun-down and I don't remember ever hearing him complain about one thing. And he never met a stranger, just had a way with people. They took to him the minute they saw him.

The old saying that opposites attract must be true because Granny was the exact opposite of Pappy. Where he had a pure zest for life, she was always waiting for the other shoe to drop. Granny hardly ever smiled. Sometimes I had the impression she didn't like farming. But maybe I'm remembering things that weren't there.

When I was thirteen Pappy bought my first guitar. He got it for ten dollars at a pawnshop in Louisville. On Saturday nights we'd sit around the potbelly stove and listen to the Grand Ole Opry on the radio and try to play along. One time, when I was fifteen, we went to the show at Renfro Valley.

But the memory that stands out the most, I think it was in the early fall of fifty-six or fifty-seven, I can't remember which, was a show that was put on from the back of a flatbed truck in a shopping center in Louisville. Sonny James was the headliner, and he sang *Young Love*. That's the moment I knew I wanted to be a star.

Read the exciting story on eBook or paperback

The Clavis Isley Story
In the
Shadow of the King

www.ingramcontent.com/pod-product-compliance
Lightning Source LLC
Chambersburg PA
CBHW060439130626
46555CB00005B/2425